INLAID TO REST

A CHARM ISLAND MYSTERY
BOOK 3

CASEY GRIFFIN

LET CASEY HAUNT YOUR INBOX

Casey Griffin's newsletter followers get access to exclusive content, fun gifts, and random shenanigans (because who doesn't love those?). You'll also receive *Dead Ringer*, a FREE NOVELLA, and be the first to hear about the next book in the series.

Sign up at
CASEYGRIFFIN.COM

CHAPTER ONE

As the speedboat bounced over waves along the rugged coastline, Alice flashed me an excited grin. I wrangled my red curls whipping in the sea breeze and returned the look, but I felt more terrified than anything. While our private boat ride to Charm Island's new resort, Siren's Call, hinted at the pampering and relaxation that awaited us, my weekend would be anything but restful, given my mission.

Since returning to my hometown a couple of months before, I'd spent a lot of time thinking about how to mend my fractured friendship with Max—I being the breaker of said friendship. I just wanted him to forgive me, for everything to go back to the way it was before I ran away from the island and, more importantly, him.

Alice giggled and gripped my arm. "This weekend is going to be amazing, isn't it, Vi? It was so nice of Trent to invite us."

Reminding myself this was still meant to be a fun weekend away with my friend, I nodded in agreement. Or at least I tried to, but my head just bobbled up and down as the boat skipped over choppy waters. "It was nice of him, but he didn't invite me. I'm your plus-one, remember? You were the one he wanted here." I waggled my eyebrows. "I wonder why."

Trent Bass, the entrepreneur and driving force behind the resort, had gathered the island's most influential residents for a sneak-peek weekend. And since Alice and I were as influential as a flea on a familiar, I suspected her invite was more personal than professional. But as the local saying went, I wasn't going to look a gift whale in the blowhole.

Her windburned cheeks turned an even brighter shade of pink. "It's professional courtesy because of my contract with Siren's Call. That's all."

"Right." I eyed her. "And what about all the time you've spent together recently?"

"He's been taste-testing the baked goods I'll be making for the resort," she argued, though it was hard to tell if it was with me or herself. "We had to finalize the menu before the grand opening next weekend. It's all totally professional."

I threw her a teasing smile. "Of course it is."

When the boat operator veered around the next rocky outcrop, the resort came into view, and I inhaled sharply. Since the last time I'd seen the place, it had transformed from a construction site to a five-story eco-friendly structure that blended into the shoreline. The perfect mix of nature and, thankfully, modern convenience. Hey, I loved the great outdoors as much as the next local, but indoor plumbing was nothing short of magical—certainly more useful than my ghost-related magic.

Alice whistled. "It's stunning."

"Definitely worth the wait," I said, scanning the marina.

I was searching for the *Crescent*, Max's blue-and-white sailboat, but vessels clogging every slip made it hard to pick out. Due to protests from local groups, the construction crew hadn't completed the forestry road from Hope yet, so traveling by sea was the best way to get to the secluded resort—a quirk that had worked in my favor.

Since my late fiancé's clingy ghost and his familiar, Zelda, hated water, I'd been able to leave them behind. Between that and taking a break from my witch studies, I had my fingers crossed for a paranormal-free weekend.

As we drew closer, I spied Max's boat, and a knot of anxiety in my stomach loosened. I'd been worried his contractor gig might have ended by now, but it seemed he was still here.

Finally. This was my chance to apologize for ghosting him for five years and to admit… what? That when he'd confessed his love for me the night before I was supposed to wed Nolan—I'd felt the same? The knot cinched again as insecurities gnawed at my resolve. What good would telling him that do?

Ever since my return, Max's behavior had made it clear that any feelings he'd had for me were in the past. As for mine? Well, it didn't matter. Obviously, my late fiancé's best friend was off limits. Especially since Nolan was still with us in spirit, and I was the lucky witch who could see him. Besides, this wasn't just about me. It was about Nolan too.

His sister had recently revealed that Max had been the last person to work on my fiancé's car. While I refused to believe he'd been responsible for sending Nolan and me off that cliff, I needed to find out what he knew. But if I wanted to build up to that conversation, I'd first have to repair our friendship, regain his trust, and fill the hole that had been residing in my chest for some time. Hopefully, this weekend would be the first step to doing that.

Once our boat puttered into a free berth, the cheerful operator helped us onto the dock before wheeling our luggage to the main building. We followed at a slower pace, our footsteps thudding along the dock with soft wooden sounds. Halfway there, a mini yacht whipped into the marina, sending its wake toward us. The wave hit the side of the dock and splashed over my shoes, soaking them.

Scowling, I watched the craft park in a space labeled "Reserved for Siren's Call Boats." A niggling sixth sense told me it was none other than Mayor Quinton Abernathy. Or maybe that was my witchy intuition kicking in, detecting another member of the local magic club. Though if that were possible, then there'd be a chance he knew I had powers, too, and I definitely didn't want that. My hunch was confirmed when His Honor disembarked and smoothed his dark hair back, accentuating his widow's peak.

Alice followed my gaze and clicked her tongue. "Well, we knew he might come. It's the downside to living on a small island. But look at the bright side."

"What's that?" I asked. "He can finally get my murder over with, and we can stop the will-he-won't-he game?"

While I understood he was a father grieving the loss of his son, I wished it didn't involve blaming me for Nolan's death. I already had that covered. And then some. Even if I managed to solve my fiancé's murder and help him move on, I wasn't sure I'd ever forgive myself for what I'd felt when Max declared his love for me. Or for the fact that my visit to his boat had been the reason Nolan and I were on the winding cliffside road that night.

Alice shot me a flat look. "No. I mean the more the Abernathys see you around, the sooner they'll accept my best friend is here to stay." She hooked her arm through mine and tugged me toward the main building as if I might run off to Europe again and never return.

I squeezed her arm but wasn't sure how to respond. Although I had a lot to accomplish on Charm Island, like learning more about my powers, reconciling with Max, and solving Nolan's murder, I wasn't sure what came after that.

At the end of the docks, we passed a two-story boathouse before continuing on to the main lodge. Automatic doors to the lobby hissed open at our approach. As we moved to enter, I caught sight of a man just as he disappeared around the corner of the building. My steps slowed. I'd have known that solid figure and saunter anywhere. Max.

Alice glanced back, already partway through the doors. "You coming?"

"I just saw Max. I should rip off the Band-Aid and say hi. Meet you inside?"

"Okay. I'll get us checked in and sign us up for spa treatments. Good luck." She gave me an encouraging thumbs-up that did nothing for my nerves. "Everything will turn out fine. You'll see."

Heart beating somewhere near my tonsils, I combed my fingers through my windblown curls and followed Max.

As I walked, my mind raced for what to say. Since my return to the island, our previous encounters had all been unavoidable run-ins, like when I'd asked him for an undeserved favor or accused him of murder. This was my first real attempt to reach out as a friend. Though "friend" felt painfully inadequate for someone who'd been central to my life since elementary school and would always hold a piece of my heart.

When I rounded the side of the building, a quiet parking lot spread out before me, sandwiched between the resort and the thick forest. I recognized Max's truck by his business logo displayed on the door, One with Nature Carpentry. He, however, was nowhere to be seen.

A moment later, the deep timbre of his voice echoed across the space. I followed his clipped words to a rusty red pickup, where he spoke with a young man in grease-stained coveralls.

Max's broad back tensed beneath his T-shirt as he tapped a clipboard against his thigh. "... and today of all days? Seriously, Levi? Are you trying to drive me out of business?"

The younger man's gaze dropped to the ground. "Of course not. I'm sorry. I forgot."

Max dragged a hand through his tousled black hair. "The inspector is going to be here soon. If we don't get the deck approved for use today, it'll be a month before we can get him back, and the grand opening is next week."

"Sorry," Levi mumbled. "I'll get those signs up right away. I swear."

Stress seemed to roll off Max in waves. Clearly, it wasn't the best time to catch up, so I decided to sneak away. Before I could, movement along the tree line caught my eye. While the thick canopy blocked out the late-morning rays, I swore something darted among the undergrowth.

I squinted against the sun. There it was again. A hint of gray and white fur, a flick of a bushy tail. Was that a wolf skulking toward us?

A strangled noise escaped me, and both men turned and stared in my direction. Wordlessly, I pointed at the forest. However, the predator was gone. Had it scurried off, or were my nerves playing tricks on me?

I blinked and scanned the woods again. "Sorry. I thought I saw…" I shook my head, feeling silly. "Never mind."

If my appearance surprised Max, he hid it well. Amusement tugged at his lips. "Violet Woods, did five years abroad turn you into a nervous tourist? I might have to revoke your islander card."

I rolled my eyes at myself. "Maybe the remote location is making me jumpy." Still, I'd mention my possible sighting to the front desk in case I hadn't imagined it. That way, they could take extra measures to protect their guests and staff.

He studied me a moment longer then focused on Levi again, his earlier irritation gone. "Get those signs up before the inspector arrives. I'm counting on you. No more mistakes today."

"Sure thing, boss." The young man jumped behind the wheel of the red pickup and leaned out the open window. "Don't worry. You can count on me."

Max struggled to maintain his composure, but an affectionate smirk slipped through. "Where have I heard that before?"

Levi turned the engine over and drove down a path to the

rocky beach. When Max's vivid blue eyes met mine, they were less welcoming than I'd hoped but not hostile, so at least there was that.

"What brings you here, Vi?"

"Trent invited Alice for the sneak peek, and she asked me to be her plus-one." I tried to sound casual despite the piranhas churning in my stomach.

"And your dad? How's his arm?"

"He's much better, thanks," I said. "The cast is off, and he's back to full-time hours at the jewelry store. It's the reason I felt comfortable taking this weekend off. I just hope he's not over-doing it."

"Knowing him, I'm sure he is."

I laughed, certain he was right. "So, what's new with you?"

He moved a little closer, and I did the same. I couldn't help but think of two magnets drawn toward each other. However, when he opened his mouth to respond, the radio clipped to his belt squawked. Levi's staticky voice came through, unintelligible to my ears.

Max pinched the bridge of his nose before keying the radio and answering him. "I'll be right there." He faced me again. "Sorry about that. Did you need something?"

His expression was one you'd expect from a DMV worker half an hour before closing, and it emphasized the rift between us. What courage I'd mustered to seek him out skittered into a dark corner.

"I came over to say hi, but it looks like I'm interrupting your work." Eager to retreat and lick my wounded ego, I started to edge away. "I'll let you get back to it. Maybe I'll see you around this weekend."

As I turned, he caught my hand, sending a jolt of electricity up my arm. When I met his gaze, the tenderness in his eyes glued my damp shoes to the ground.

"Let's catch up at the party tonight," he said. "It's been too long."

Some of my earlier hope fluttered in my stomach. "Sure. I'll see you there." I backed away. "Oh, and watch out for wolves in the area."

He stiffened. "Wolves?"

"Yeah. I swore I saw one lurking out there." I nodded to the tree line. When his look grew even darker, I grinned. "Now who's acting like a scared tourist?"

After a beat, he remembered to chuckle. "Right. Thanks for the warning."

His demeanor came off as forced, and I wanted to press him about it, but things were going well so far, and I didn't want to ruin that. Perhaps he was just feeling as awkward about our interaction as I was—I had caught him off guard after all. So I waved goodbye and headed for the lobby.

Alice met me halfway down the path, grinning as she jingled a set of keys. "Trent upgraded us to a private cabin. Can you believe it? This is going to be a magical weekend."

I held up a hand. "Don't jinx me. I'm hoping to avoid all things magical. Let's just have a relaxing weekend."

Once I'd slipped my arm through hers, I peered back over my shoulder for one last look at Max. He appeared lost in thought as he studied the woods like he was searching for signs of the predator. But he didn't look worried. In fact, his expression seemed to say the wolf should be.

CHAPTER TWO

While Alice and I got ready for the sunset party, I marveled at our private cabin. From the outside, it looked rustic, with its rich brown log exterior and green roof camouflaging it into the landscape. However, the inside screamed five-star luxury, complete with a peaked ceiling, chandeliers, and chic yet comfortable furniture. The inviting ambience tempted me to skip the party and stay in with room service. Though that might have had more to do with my nerves over seeing Max again.

As Alice and I stepped out of the cabin and set out for the main lodge, the cool evening air formed goose bumps on my skin. My ballet flats didn't exactly match my sleek black cocktail dress, but heels didn't seem appropriate for the rugged surroundings either—especially after my earlier wolf sighting. It would be annoying to get eaten alive because my choice in footwear prevented a quick escape.

The second Alice and I entered the lobby, the low hum of pleasant conversation and distant music beckoned us up a suspended staircase. We followed a two-story waterfall feature to the top, where lively chatter accosted us. More than a hundred guests loitered in the open-concept space or took in the colorful sunset from the large wooden deck. My focus shifted from one well-dressed guest to another, but Max wasn't among them.

Anxious to find him, I kept an eye out as Alice and I drifted through the room, taking in the splendor. My chest fluttered with anticipation, a conflicting mix of eagerness to finally hash things out with him and simmering dread over no longer being able to avoid it.

The atmosphere buzzed with excitement and curiosity, but as we passed people sipping cocktails and nibbling hors d'oeu-vres, I overheard a few scathing comments about our host and the accommodations.

"It's too bright with all these windows," one muttered. "I can't see where I'm going."

Another sniffed. "Would it have killed them to have more wine options?"

Considering the extravagance of the place and the huge seafood buffet—plus the fact it was all free—I was surprised at the guests' prickly moods. It wasn't the vibe I'd expected from people elbow-deep in lobster and luxury.

Alice clutched my arm. "Look, there's Trent."

I spotted the man wearing a tailor-made navy blue suit headed straight for us. He was laser-focused on Alice as though his VIP had arrived. While I'd only met him once before, he seemed like a stand-up guy. However, in my recent experience, even stand-up people were capable of murder. But how often could that happen on a small island, right?

He spread his arms out in welcome. "Alice, Violet. I'm so glad you made it."

Alice beamed. "We wouldn't have missed it for the world."

"Thank you for the invitation," I said.

"Of course. I'm just happy to have two friendly faces in the crowd this weekend." His eyes darted to a few of the less friendly ones I'd noted on our arrival, but his excitement hardly faltered. "Some locals are still opposed to the resort. I've invited the most vocal critics, hoping to mend fences and build new friendships, but I think I've got my work cut out for me this weekend."

I guessed that explained the friction I'd detected in the room.

Alice bounced on the balls of her feet. "I know just the thing to help you. I'll sneak into the kitchen tomorrow and bake something special for you, if you'll allow it, of course. You'd be surprised at how a homemade cookie can work magic on stress."

I suppressed a snort, knowing she meant magic in the literal sense. Alice had recently learned she was a kitchen witch and, since she was a quicker study than I was, had come a long way in controlling the emotions of her taste testers. It was terrifying when I really thought about it, but thankfully she used her powers for good and kept the effects mild.

As Trent licked his lips at the mention of her famous baking, a young woman in a blue A-line dress materialized at his elbow. She appeared to be a few years younger than my twenty-seven. But while she looked as if she belonged on a runway, she hugged her tablet like all she wanted to do was run away.

"Sorry to interrupt," she squeaked.

"Penelope, there you are." Trent stepped aside to allow her into our little circle. "Alice, Violet, this is Penelope, my assistant. Well, miracle worker is a more accurate job title."

A smile lit her angelic face, revealing perfect teeth, before she self-consciously covered them with a manicured hand. Her electric-blue nails were a striking contrast to the blush creeping across her flawless skin. "Miracle worker's a bit of a stretch. I went to school for architecture," she told us. "After graduation, I was lucky to get my foot in Trent's door."

"She's being modest," he said. "We wouldn't be here without her. When I was first contemplating this project, she told me about Charm Island. And once I visited, I couldn't pass up a gem like this."

"Have you spent time here before?" Alice asked her.

"I'm originally from the island. I've always thought it was a shame more people don't know about it. A place this beautiful should be shared with the world. It's so… untouched, like Bigfoot might be hiding in your backyard. It's magical."

If only she knew. There was more than one paranormal being on the island, but it wasn't Bigfoot. As far as I knew, anyway.

She turned back to Trent. "Speaking of magic, everyone seems to be here now, so you could work some of yours with a welcome speech whenever you're ready."

He checked his watch. "I guess it's that time. Please, excuse me," he told Alice and me. "I'll catch up with you later."

As he hurried off with Penelope in tow, we approached the beverage table, where artisanal cocktails formed the tail of a mermaid ice sculpture. I selected a drink that was more garnish than liquid, and Alice did the same. We'd barely taken our first sips when Trent's voice rose above the din.

"Welcome, everyone!"

The crowd shuffled as one to where he stood in front of the floor-to-ceiling windows. We moved with the flow of bodies and found a spot near the buffet table. Backlit by the sunset, Trent's dark-blond waves blushed pink. He was young for someone so successful, maybe early thirties, but in his excitement, his boyish grin made him seem younger.

He waited until the chatter and clicking heels hushed. "For those of you who don't know me, I'm Trent Bass. I'm so grateful you all accepted my invitation. Many of you have helped see this project come to fruition, and I'm looking forward to showing you my appreciation this weekend. Of course, there are some of you who have been, shall we say, resistant to the resort."

A wiry man to my left guffawed. "That's an understatement."

I eyed my disgruntled neighbor. He popped shrimp into his mouth like popcorn at a movie, and judging by the ironic twist to his lips, this was a dark comedy. I didn't see what was so funny.

Hardly batting an eyelash, Trent carried on, touching on the resort's eco-friendly features. He exuded an effortless charm as naturally as most people exuded sweat on a treadmill, and guests leaned in with interest. But he wasn't charming everyone. A few mirrored my neighbor's sour attitude, muttering sarcastic comments about the location or throwing scathing looks at their grandiose surroundings.

I couldn't blame them, since I'd had my own reservations when I first visited the place. Though the resort would draw more tourists and boost the local economy, the trade-off was losing part of the island's wild, untamed quality. It made me think of how Max, Nolan, and I used to explore hidden inlets on the *Crescent*, feeling as if we'd stepped into another world, one where only the three of us existed. The presence of a big resort would bring that daydream crashing back to Earth. But with my family's business teetering on the edge of closure, I could sympathize with both sides of the argument. The situation was anything but black and white.

Amid the mixed reviews, Trent concluded his speech. "Please, don't hesitate to approach me with any questions you might have, and I hope you enjoy yourselves this weekend."

"Ha!" my neighbor barked. "Fat chance of that happening."

Guests gave a smattering of applause before returning to their previous conversations. Some approached Trent to shake his hand, and one eager woman with golden hair pushed her way past them all.

"Mr. Bass, can I get a photo for my article?" Lucy Litton's distinct voice pierced the air like shattering glass.

As though this were a red-carpet event, she'd worn a sequined dress and fake-fur shrug. At least, I hoped it was fake with all the nature and wildlife surrounding us. Then again, Lucy had never been good at reading the room.

While I wasn't thrilled to see her there, I should have expected Hope's hungriest reporter to score an invitation. At least she wasn't hounding me. For once.

I nudged Alice's arm. "I'm going to get another drink. Why don't you go over and talk to Trent again?"

She hugged herself. "He seems busy. I don't want to interrupt."

"Since he's busy with Lucy, I'm sure he wouldn't mind. Besides, you don't want to waste a dress like that." I gestured to her off-the-shoulder number.

She gnawed on her bottom lip. "I think I will. You know, to thank him for upgrading our room."

"I know. I know. Professional courtesy and all that." I shooed her away. "You two will have a very professional wedding."

She flashed me a wry look before crossing the room.

As I watched her go, a business card appeared in front of my face. I flinched and stared at the person holding it. The man who'd heckled Trent.

"Don't be shy." He waved the card at me.

I took it and read the name to myself. "Leonard Crab: owner and operator of The Shipwreck Shelter."

It took me a moment to place the business name. Then the rundown motel near Hope's cannery came to mind—the one with a faded sign missing a couple of letters, like it had given up trying to attract customers. The only reason it was still in business was because, aside from a few B and B's, the island had little in the way of competition. Until now.

He puffed up his chest. "If you ever want to stay at a real

hotel and not this stuffy place, call me. There's a discount on the back of the card."

I flipped it over. Sure enough, it doubled as a coupon for ten percent off my next stay. Which would be… never. Given a choice between staying at his infamous roach motel and an actual shipwreck, I would have chosen the latter.

Eyeing the seafood spread behind me, he grabbed a new plate. "If you'll excuse me. They just brought out fresh prawns, and I don't want to miss them. Have you had any yet? I mean, they're all right," he said in a take-it-or-leave-it kind of way while emptying the serving dish onto his plate. "Nothing beats my wife's cooking, but free food is free food."

"Er, no. I haven't had the chance to try them." And at the rate he was going, I didn't think anyone else would either.

"Gotta take advantage while I can." He sampled a California roll then balanced several of them on his loaded plate. "After all, this place won't be around for long."

I frowned. "What do you mean?"

"No one's going to stay all the way out here." He indicated the resort with a wave of a crab leg. "Tourists don't want to be this far away from all the action."

I wasn't sure what "action" Hope had, but the boats bobbing in the marina suggested guest transport wouldn't be an issue. "I think they're trying to attract clientele who want to get away from it all."

"They'll want to get away, all right. Get away from this dump, that is. And I'll be happy to take their reservations." Clearly pleased with his marketing efforts, he continued to survey the buffet table.

Before he ran out of room on his plate and tried to rope me back into the conversation, I subtly tossed his card into a nearby garbage can and headed to the bar for a drink. My steps faltered when I spotted Quinton Abernathy sipping a scotch. His discerning gaze swept over the grand room as though searching for flaws—a scuff on the hardwood floor, perhaps, or a burned-out light bulb in the chandeliers. Finally, his focus landed on me, and his lip curled into a sneer. Apparently, I hadn't passed the inspection.

To avoid him, I veered toward the opposite end of the bar. Leaning against the live-edge wood slab, I tried to catch the nearest bartender's attention. When she turned, sweeping her long braids away from her pretty face, I lost my desire for a drink. It was Roxy, Max's, er… friend.

I'd forgotten the resort had hired her as bar manager. In fact, if I'd remembered, I might have reconsidered coming on the trip at all. I hadn't exactly made the best impression on her when I first returned to the island, and our last conversation had been more than a little awkward, with me accusing her of murder and all.

As she approached, a ruby pendant sparkled against her dark skin, matching the shock of red braided into her hair. The necklace Max had given her. When I'd questioned him about it —because it was a key piece of evidence and totally not because I was jealous—he'd told me it was a gesture of friendship. But perhaps things had changed between them since they'd been working closely together at the resort.

Pushing the thought aside, I wiggled my fingers as she approached. "Hi, Roxy."

When she recognized me, her dark eyes cooled before she plastered on a polite expression. "Violet. What can I get you?"

"Vodka soda with a lime, please."

As she grabbed a glass, it occurred to me the only times we'd ever talked was when I ordered a drink or questioned her about a murder. I searched for a safer topic.

"So, how do you like the new job?"

She plucked a bottle of vodka from the shelf behind her. "So far, it's been slow. This weekend is my first real test."

"Do you enjoy working this far out of town?"

"It's a different world from Killer Ale but a nice change.

I'm still trying to figure out where I belong on the island. I want to find a pack to run with, you know?"

Given her history, I didn't blame her. She'd come to Charm Island for one tourist season and ended up staying for a manipulative man who'd turned out to be a thief—a profession that led to his untimely death.

She plopped a straw and a slice of lime into my drink before sliding the glass in front of me. "Anyway. Enjoy the party."

It wasn't clear if her brusque dismissal was because she needed to serve the next customer or if she wanted to be rid of me. Either way, I wasn't about to complain. I'd made nice and wasn't eager to hang around her or Abernathy, who seemed intent on sampling the entire top shelf.

Feeling out of place, I wandered over to the wall of windows to take in the sinking sun. Half submerged beneath the ocean, it set the sky ablaze. As I appreciated the breathtaking view, I spied a large figure approach at the edge of my vision. Hoping for Max, my heart leaped, but it turned out to be a man I'd never seen before.

While his sturdy figure bore a resemblance to my friend, as did the way he carried himself, he was older, mid-forties. And where Max was all hard lines and chiseled angles, this stranger's muscles nestled deeper, as though they'd made themselves at home for longer. Dressed in jeans and a button-up plaid shirt that stretched over his broad shoulders, he stuck out among the crowd. Apparently, he'd missed the memo about the semiformal dress code.

His friendly smile flashed beneath a trimmed beard. "Beautiful view, isn't it?"

"It is," I agreed. "The best sunset I've ever seen on the island." And that was saying something.

"Seems a shame to ruin it with this monstrosity." He gestured at our surroundings with a half-empty glass.

"I take it you're not a fan."

"Not exactly." He held out a calloused hand. "I'm Garrett Swift."

"Violet Woods." As I shook his hand, my attention—or my powers—homed in on his silver ring. The inlaid black stone bore an intricate symbol I longed to study, but whether it was my professional curiosity or the lingering spirits of its past owners calling to my magic, it wasn't the time or place. "If you're not a fan of Siren's Call, what brings you here this weekend? The complimentary pedicures?"

His mouth twitched in amusement. "I'm here because Trent is trying to win me over. You see, I'm the leader of a village called Truce."

I nearly sloshed my drink onto my dress. "The same Truce that's been behind all the protests?" I guessed that explained his outfit. It was like he was mocking the chic affair, protesting until the bitter end.

He chuckled at my surprise, a warm and inviting sound. "Let's just say I've come with a few concerns about the resort's impact on our village."

"Lucy has written some articles about your protests, but she usually embellishes. I'm curious to hear your side of things."

Facing the window, Garrett pointed north, to the farthest tip of the inlet where Sleeping Beauty Mountain fanned out like tendrils of hair cascading from a woman lying on her side. "Truce is located beyond that first ridge. We rely on hunting and fishing for food. Introducing a horde of tourists and boat activity to the area would disturb the wildlife."

I nodded. "That makes sense."

"Not to mention, we don't want any stray hikers stumbling into our village. We're a private bunch, so we like to keep to ourselves."

Someone scoffed behind us, and we spun to find Max sauntering our way. While his well-fitted suit said he'd come prepared for a good time, the scowl he aimed at the other man told a different story.

"It's true," he told me. "Garrett doesn't get out much, but that's to everyone's advantage."

He planted himself between me and my new acquaintance, almost protectively. The sun's last blazing stand against the night made him appear as if he were on fire, and when the Truce leader squared off with him, it seemed things were about to heat up.

CHAPTER THREE

Garrett and Max sized each other up like two alphas preparing for a brawl over territory. Hopefully, that territory was the resort and not me, because I was no one's property.

"I take it you two know each other," I said to break the tension.

Garrett huffed a lazy laugh. "You could say that."

It shouldn't have come as a surprise, since Max had grown up in Truce, though he'd rarely talk about it. The first rule of being from the village seemed to be that you didn't talk about it. But one thing went without saying: these two men had some serious history.

I'd been so caught up in the showdown that I hadn't noticed two other guests approach until they stood on either side of the village leader. One was a short, muscular man with close-set eyes. The other was a tall woman with a pixie cut so blond it appeared almost white. Garrett's friends, I supposed. However, based on their tense stances and the way they flanked him, bodyguards would have been a better word. Not that he looked like he needed anyone to fight his battles.

Max crossed his arms over his sturdy chest. "What are you doing here, Garrett? I hope you're not searching for trouble."

"Who, me?" he asked way too innocently. "I'm an invited guest. I came to make peace with Trent."

Max narrowed his eyes. "I have a hard time believing that after all the problems you've caused this place."

"Allegedly," the woman added with an ironic quirk to her eyebrow. The thin white scar slashing through it lent a sharper edge to her derision.

Garrett raised an indifferent shoulder. "Well, Max. It's a good thing I don't care what traitors think."

Traitors? What did that mean? Questions flooded my mouth, but the others seemed to have forgotten I was there. Wanting to keep it that way, I bit my tongue.

"Excuse me," a female voice squeaked nearby. "I hope I'm not interrupting."

We all shifted to regard Penelope, who smiled sweetly, as though a rabbit had hopped into the middle of a grizzly bear brawl. No one seemed to know what to say. Garrett looked especially stunned.

"Welcome to Siren's Call. I'm not sure if you remember me. I'm Penelope, Mr. Bass's assistant." She held out a hand to Garrett. When he didn't move, she dropped her hand and scrolled down a list on her tablet. "I'm sorry I haven't welcomed you yet. We didn't receive your RSVP, so I assumed you weren't attending. I see you checked in this afternoon into a mountain-view suite. I'd be happy to upgrade you and your friends to a private cabin."

"Thanks," Garrett said. "But we're comfortable where we are."

The compact man next to him shifted. "I wouldn't mind a private cabin."

"Shut it, Shane," Garrett shot back.

"Trent will be thrilled you changed your mind," Penelope told him. "He's right this way if you'd like to say hello."

The suggestion gave him a way out of the heated situation with Max and an opportunity to prove he was there to "make peace with Trent." Even so, I thought he'd brush it off.

After a beat, his rigid posture relaxed. "Lead the way." He raised his glass to me. "Maybe I'll see you around this weekend."

With a smirk at Max, he ambled away, his solid friend following close on his heel. The blond woman lingered, but it wasn't Max who held her focus. Instead, she gave me a once-over, her scarred eyebrow twitching with judgment.

While I got the sense she knew me, I'd never seen her before. I would have remembered her, if not for her sunny disposition, then for her distinct choice in accessories. A series of polished silver bracelets clung to her forearms like ornate sleeves, detailed images etched into the metal.

Garrett glanced back. "Teagan, you coming?" It sounded like an order rather than a question.

She obeyed but not before she bared her teeth at me. I guessed that was a warning to keep away. I was happy to do so.

When they'd gone, I swiveled to face Max, who was still glaring at Garrett's back. I didn't want whatever had just happened to ruin the evening, so I searched for a way to snap him out of his mood. "I haven't seen you that worked up since Cory Hansen shoved a dissected frog down my sweater in high school."

The memory broke whatever spell he was under, and the scowl slipped from his face. "The frog." He groaned. "That's right. Cory was such a jerk. I hated that guy."

"You don't say? The black eye you gave him got you suspended for a week."

The corner of his mouth curled up. "Worth it."

I bit back a grin. "But I don't think Garrett is carrying any frogs, so want to tell me what that was all about?"

He released a long breath. "It's complicated."

While I knew how to break his bad moods, I also knew that when he didn't want to talk, no amount of prodding would get him to open up, so I let it go. "Why would Trent invite anyone from Truce, much less their leader?"

He shrugged. "The same reason he invited many resistant locals. To offer an olive branch."

I looked across the room to where Penelope was introducing the group to her boss. "Do you think Garrett's here to take it?"

"Not for a second." His expression tightened, but after a moment, he shifted his shoulders as though shaking off the encounter. "Come on. Let's get some fresh air."

My stomach flipped like I was a high school girl with a crush. This was the moment I'd been hoping for. Now that it was here, though, my heart fluttered so fast it stole my breath, along with my voice, so I simply nodded.

I set my drink on a nearby table and followed him through the open French doors onto the deck that stood two stories off the ground. Bypassing guests chatting beneath string lights, we found a quiet spot along the railing, away from everyone else. The unobstructed view of the sunset was magnificent. Far below, the low tide exposed the beach sloping away from the lodge, and strips of drying seaweed clung to the colorful rocks.

As Max stared out at the inlet, the muscles in his jaw worked. He'd shaved for the event—a rare sight—and I couldn't help but notice how nicely he cleaned up. Over the last five years, he'd lost some of that youthful softness, as though time had chiseled away at him. The man who remained was harder and more defined, both physically and emotionally.

The silence stretched, and I felt like my chance to talk openly with him was slipping away. Since Nolan's ghost usually followed me everywhere, I didn't know when we'd get another opportunity to chat without him overhearing something he shouldn't, and the last thing I wanted was to hurt my fiancé.

While nothing had ever happened between Max and me, Nolan would be heartbroken to learn about his best friend's confession of love. And if he confronted me about it, I wasn't certain I could hide my true feelings.

As a ghost, he was trapped in a single moment in time—the night before our wedding, at the height of our romantic relationship. I imagined finding out would cut him as deeply as if it had happened yesterday. No matter how many years passed, he'd never let go of our love, of me.

Still finding my footing with Max, I decided I'd need to build up to the heavier subjects, so I started with small talk. "So, do you have any more carpentry jobs lined up after you're done here?"

"Actually, I've already completed the contract for the resort. Trent asked me to stay on as a maintenance worker until he can find someone permanent. While it's not my ideal job, there isn't always an abundance of work on the island."

"What about your photography? Alice mentioned you don't do it anymore, but it would make a good side hustle. You were so talented."

He waved off the compliment. "I still snap the odd photo. It'll never pay the bills, though. Carpentry is stable, and I still get to be creative."

"Well, from what I've seen in our cabin, you do amazing work."

"Thanks." He rubbed the back of his neck. "Anyway, I'm sure you have more to talk about, what with your travels through Europe."

I let out a breath that was just as much a laugh as a sigh. "Where to start? The food, the architecture, not to mention the antique jewelry hidden in obscure shops, ripe for the picking."

He leaned against the railing as if settling in to hear more. "Where was your favorite place?"

"I can't pick just one. I went where the wind took me and moved on when it was time for the next adventure."

My smile wavered a little. The truth was, I'd never been ready to leave any of my destinations, but I'd had no choice.

Once one ghost discovered my ability to see them, word would spread fast, and they'd follow me wherever I went. I supposed they'd thought I could help them move on. My local fan base would grow until I wasn't able to take a shower without an audience, then I'd find the nearest body of water to cross, leaving them all in my wake. Thankfully, water was a universal ghost deterrent, and they never followed.

As I recounted some of my happier memories, Max's mood shifted. I sensed it—not with my magic but the subtler, intangible connection we'd always shared. I took in his stiff posture and the tension tugging at the corners of his eyes. Worried I was talking too much, I stopped rambling.

"Sounds like you had a great time," he said. "When you've got the Louvre and the Colosseum, what's there to miss about Charm Island?"

I caught the bitterness in his voice, and my insides twisted. Was he suggesting I hadn't missed him? I wished he understood how far from the truth that was. There were so many things I wanted to confess.

It seemed small talk was over, which was fine with me; it had felt awkward and so not "us." While Nolan and I had never run out of things to say when he was alive, Max and I had always connected differently, saying much more without talking at all. And when we did, it had been real talk, the hard stuff—though with him, it never felt hard.

"If you recall, my extended trip wasn't the honeymoon I'd planned," I said quietly.

"I know. Sorry. I shouldn't have brought it up."

His focus dropped to the railing and froze on my hand. I followed his gaze and realized what he was staring at. My wedding ring. I'd grown so used to wearing it that I hadn't thought to take it off before leaving home.

At first, having the band on had felt strange, even on my right hand. But jewelry connected to a soul acted as a conduit for my magic—one of the many quirks of my powers I was still learning about. Without the ring, I wouldn't be able to hear Nolan speak, and other than Zelda, I was the only one who could hear or see ghosts. I always wore it so he'd have someone to talk to.

Max regarded it before turning away with a grimace. Did he think I wore it because I wasn't over Nolan's death? Well, I supposed in a way, I wasn't. And I never would be until I helped his spirit move on.

I wondered how much to tell Max. We'd been so close. Even though he was human, could I tell him I was a witch, that I'd left because Nolan had haunted me mere hours after his death? Or perhaps it was better to stick to something easier, like the unspoken apology that had been sitting on my chest for five years.

"Max, listen. I—"

"Wait." He gripped my arm, attention flitting around the deck.

I opened my mouth to ask what was wrong, but an ominous groan filled the air like an out-of-tune cello.

Crack.

The sound of snapping wood stopped my heart. Then the deck shifted beneath my shoes. It was collapsing.

"Everyone, get inside!" Max yelled, steering me toward the French doors.

Cries rose from those outside, punctuated by the sounds of splintering wood. Panic closed around my throat as I imagined the two-story fall beneath our feet.

The other guests were closer to the doors and quickly squeezed into the building. Hovering just inside the threshold, they clutched their pearls—sometimes literally—watching with wide eyes as Max and I ran from our far corner of the deck.

His grip on my arm tightened with the strength of a python as he pulled me along like a lifeline. I prayed he wouldn't let go. We were almost there. Then the planks beneath us heaved.

Chunks of wood flew like shrapnel, and the world tilted as though we were running uphill. It was no good. We were still too far away.

Max pressed his hand firmly against my back and pushed me to safety. Arms pinwheeling, I surged toward the doors. People grabbed whatever part of me they could—arms, dress, hair—and yanked me inside.

I collapsed on the floor and watched with relief as Max tumbled in after me. A second later, the last of the massive deck crashed to the exposed rocky beach.

CHAPTER FOUR

Legs trembling, I rose to my feet and peered at the wreckage on the rocks far below. The waves licked at the shattered remains of the once-beautiful deck, now an unrecognizable pile of twisted metal and broken wood. I didn't know how Max had gotten us to safety, but if he hadn't, I'd have been down there, just as twisted and unrecognizable.

Max grabbed me by the shoulders, turning me to face him. "Are you okay?"

"I-I think so," I said. "Thanks to you. How did you react so quickly? I was still trying to figure out what the noise was when you hauled me to the door."

"It was no big deal." He dropped his gaze from mine. "Quick reflexes, I guess."

People gathered around, their exclamations and agitated chatter rippling back to those craning their necks at the edge of the crowd. Their faces held a mix of horror and shock, but it was hard to take the near-death experience seriously when the soundtrack was an upbeat jazz number blasting through the speakers. After a moment, someone stopped the tunes, and my anxiety skyrocketed.

Mayor Abernathy stormed over to assess the scene.

"What's going on here?" When his eyes landed on me, they narrowed. "What did you do?"

Scowling, I mentally prepared a sharp retort. However, Trent pushed to the front of the throng, interrupting me—which was probably for the best.

"Is anyone hurt?" He scanned the guests closest to the doors. "What on earth happened?"

Penelope was on his heels. "Does anyone need an ambulance?"

Max stepped forward, palms raised. "The deck collapsed, but everyone's okay."

Maybe paranoia was getting the best of me, but as Abernathy eyed me, I swore he looked disappointed. I knew for a fact he would have taken pleasure in my demise—he'd told me so on more than one occasion.

"Speak for yourself," an older woman told Max. "I'm not okay. I'll be having nightmares for months."

Abernathy snapped his fingers and demanded a chair as though it would appear by magic. Who knew? Perhaps it would. I still had no idea what his powers entailed—Nolan refused to tell me, treating it like a national secret. When another guest dragged a seat over, the woman sank onto it, fanning herself with a hand.

"Mrs. Goodrich," Abernathy cooed in a way he reserved for campaign donors. "I'm so sorry. I'm sure there is a good explanation for this incident." The look he aimed at Trent said there'd better be.

Trent stiffened, and the color drained from his face. "I don't understand. The building inspector was here this morning to approve the deck for use."

A derisive snort sounded nearby. We all turned to find Leonard Crab brandishing a plate of seafood at the deck—or, rather, the lack of one. "Maybe it's thanks to shoddy workmanship. I mean, this place has had one problem after another since construction began. Something like this was bound to happen."

Abernathy fixed the man with a dark glare. "You'd know about shoddy workmanship, wouldn't you, Leonard? We've all seen your hotel."

Chuckles rose from the crowd, and Leonard ducked his head. He kept any further comments to himself, wisely choosing to stuff his mouth with prawns.

Max was staring at the open doors, his brows knitted in concentration. Finally, he seemed to come to some decision and approached them. Phone in hand, he leaned out over the empty void to assess the side of the building. My chest tightened as he gripped the doorframe with one hand and snapped photos with the other.

As I watched, Alice slipped through the crowd and rushed to my side. When she threw her arms around me, I remained in her embrace until my trembling settled. While she was a kitchen witch, I swore her powers extended to her presence. It was more effective on my stress than the three hours we'd spent in the spa that afternoon.

When Max returned, he showed Trent a picture he'd taken with his phone. "The joists connecting the deck to the building have split too cleanly."

"Meaning?" Abernathy asked.

"Meaning they were cut intentionally."

Alice clapped a hand over her mouth. "You mean someone did this on purpose?"

Murmurs rippled through the crowd. The word "sabotage" was volleyed about as whispered theories emerged.

"Why didn't the inspector catch the damage?" Trent asked.

Max rubbed his fingers together. A fine, light powder coated them. "There's still sawdust on the joists. We had a downpour last night, and it only let up this morning. If somebody had made the cuts before then, the sawdust would have washed away. My guess is it was done after the inspection."

Trent pressed a palm to his forehead. "Why would someone do this?"

"Better question is who?" A voice sliced through the chatter. When the crowd parted again, Lucy Litton sashayed over to us. "This place is too remote to hike in by foot. And the staff would have noticed another vehicle or boat arrive." She looked at Trent for confirmation.

He shrugged, a dazed expression on his face. "No one reported any unexpected visitors to me."

Alice drew in a sharp breath. "So whoever did it could be in this room, drinking champagne, right now?"

Mrs. Goodrich regarded Leonard with a curl to her lip. "Or eating half the seafood spread."

The hotel owner jerked, a crab leg pausing halfway to his lips. "And what's that supposed to mean? Why would I have done this?"

"Come on." She scoffed. "We all know you hate Siren's Call. I'm sure you'd love to see this place shut down for building code violations."

"Why are you blaming me? I haven't been the one forming picket lines since day one." He pointed the crab leg in Garrett's direction.

The Truce leader crossed his arms, and his two friends shifted as if readying for a fight. Teagan, the tall blond woman, bared her teeth like she'd done to me. It reminded me of an animal giving warning before an attack. Leonard shrank back, but he'd succeeded in redirecting everyone's scrutiny to Truce.

Garrett lifted a single shoulder. "Truce has always protested peacefully."

"Until now," Lucy chimed in. "The resort is about to open, and you've run out of time. Maybe you were feeling desperate."

I stepped forward, holding up my hands. "Hold on, everyone. Before we point more fingers, did anyone witness something? I mean, cutting the posts and beams under the deck would have taken time and tools."

Leonard raised a finger in the air. "That reminds me. While kayaking today, I saw a red truck parked by the deck."

"That would have been my worker, Levi," Max said. "He was doing a last-minute job before the inspection."

Garrett cocked his head to the side. "So you're saying Levi had both the access and the tools to sabotage it?"

Teagan's focus snapped to her leader, and she gave him a questioning look. Her lips parted as though ready to argue, then she clamped them together.

Garrett didn't notice or at least pretended not to. "Plus, Levi has a shady past. He even got arrested once for a break and enter. But you know all about that, don't you, Max?"

Max's eyes blazed as he stared the other man down. The muscles in Teagan's jaw flexed, her chest rising and falling faster. Whatever the "complicated" history between them, Levi was obviously wrapped up in it too.

Despite the tense atmosphere, Trent stepped between them. "Everyone, please! I have faith in the people who work for me. Now, that's enough speculation. It's not our job to find the culprit. It's the sheriff's." He made eye contact with Penelope. "Can you please have the bar staff shut down for the night? Then, contact Sheriff Reed and prepare the security footage for him to review. I want this sorted out as soon as possible."

With a nod, she hugged her tablet so tight I thought it might crack and disappeared into the crowd.

The debate over, the gathering dispersed. Perhaps no one wanted to wait around for the sheriff, especially now that the bar was closed. However, if Lucy's theory held true and the culprit lurked among us, this was their opportunity to make themselves scarce.

Restless, I turned back to Max to discover he'd also snuck off. I scanned the room and spotted him by the bar, talking to

Roxy with their heads bent close. As he raked a hand through his shaggy hair, she gave him a hug, and he lingered in her embrace. Jealousy popped up inside my chest like a Jack-in-the-box, but I shoved it back down.

After what felt like forever, he slipped away from the bar. As he made his way to the exit, I wasn't the only one watching him. Other curious gazes followed his progress across the room, including Lucy's sharp eagle eyes. People whispered behind their hands, likely resuming their earlier speculations.

I squeezed Alice's arm. "I'll meet up with you later, okay?"

Before she could respond, I chased after Max. I caught up to him at the top of the staircase and tugged on his sleeve. "Where are you going?"

"To look for Levi," he said. "The sheriff will have questions for him. So do I."

"I'm coming with you."

"No, Vi. I—"

I linked my arm with his and led him down the stairs like we were going for a casual walk. "This way, it'll look like we're getting some fresh air after our nerve-racking experience. If you go off alone, it will seem suspicious."

"Good point." His tense arm muscles melted beneath my touch. "And the company wouldn't be so bad either."

Did he mean any company or my company specifically? I shook it off. *Inappropriate time, Vi.*

It wasn't how I'd imagined getting closer to Max, but if I wanted to spend more time with him, this was as good an opportunity as any. And most importantly, I wanted to be there for him, both to support him and to keep him out of trouble if he ran into Garrett. I only hoped when we tracked Levi down, he could prove he'd had nothing to do with the deck.

CHAPTER FIVE

When Max and I stepped outside, the only light gracing the sky came from the nearly full moon and its starry friends. The chilly air sucked the heat from my exposed skin, and I rubbed my bare arms. I wished I'd brought a wrap to the party. However, I'd been expecting cocktails and dancing, not an impromptu manhunt.

As if reading my mind, Max slid off his suit coat and held it out for me. I thanked him and slipped into it, soaking up the warmth from his body that clung to the fabric. My nose tingled from his earthy scent, and I subtly turned my head to his collar and inhaled the mixture of pine needles and cedar.

When we reached the parking lot, he pointed out Levi's red pickup at the far end. "His vehicle is still here, so he must be too."

"When did you last see him?"

He pursed his lips as he thought. "When the inspector signed off on the deck. I felt bad for riding him so hard this morning, so I told him to take the rest of the day off once he'd cleaned up his tools. Later on, I saw his truck parked in the lot and looked for him to apologize but never found him. I assumed he returned to his cabin and decided to give him some space."

I laid a hand on his shoulder. "I'm sure you two will work things out. Which way is his cabin?"

He tilted his head to the other side of the lot. "The employee housing is over there."

I was about to tell him to lead the way when movement drew my attention. Something slunk along the edge of the forest, beyond the pools of light from the lampposts. A wolf.

A gasp escaped me, and I backpedaled right into Max.

He gripped me by the arms. "What's wrong? What do you see?"

I pointed at the advancing animal, noting its gray fur and the band of white encircling its neck as though it were a cowl. It looked like the same one I'd warned the front desk about.

Max's focus slid right over the spot where the wolf lurked, but he didn't react. As it stepped out of the shadows, form fading beneath the lights, I cursed myself for not realizing sooner. It was a ghost.

It annoyed me that despite all the work I'd been doing with my neighbor and witchy mentor, Helen, and occasionally Zelda, I still couldn't tell the difference between the living and the dead. Not without direct light, anyway.

Gathering myself, I pulled away from Max. "Sorry. I thought I saw something in the trees. It must have been my imagination. Let's go check Levi's cabin."

Max didn't move. "If being out here makes you nervous, you don't have to come with me. It's okay if you want to go back to your room."

"I'm fine. Really."

The concerned look lingered before he nodded and cut a path across the parking lot. I stayed close, monitoring the phantom wolf that shadowed us. It wasn't lurking but trotting at a jaunty pace, yet it still unnerved me.

Zelda had once explained that anything with a soul could

leave a ghost behind, including animals, though I'd only ever come across one. However, unlike humans, their unfinished business was usually simple—a bird catching a last worm, a squirrel storing one final nut—and then they'd quickly move on. So why was this one hanging around?

We walked deeper onto the property, and the forest closed in around us. Just as quickly, it spat us out into a clearing where a collection of log cabins hid from sight. Clothes hung from wires between them, and muddy hiking boots dried on porches. While smaller than the guest cabins and lacking an ocean view, they held a certain rustic charm.

Max approached one with a darkened interior and rapped on the door. As we waited in silence, I strained my ears for sounds of movement within, but it was dead quiet.

With a sigh, he descended the porch steps. "Come on. He might be blowing off steam with the other staff."

I followed him across a grassy field littered with volleyball and soccer nets. Our footsteps swished loudly, unlike those of our furry stalker, who trailed us like we had steaks in our back pockets. Up ahead, a simple one-story building sprawled across the clearing, and judging by the rowdy cheers and music drifting out, I assumed it was an employee common area.

The noisy facility threw our silence into contrast, and I started working through potential theories to fill it. "Max, is there a chance Levi did something to the deck? I mean, he is from Truce, and the people there have tried everything to derail the resort. Maybe he feels more strongly about it than you realize."

He gave a firm shake of his head. "Levi might be several years younger than me, but we grew up together. I know him. There's no way."

"What makes you so sure?" I pressed. "Garrett said something about him having a rough past."

He threw me a sidelong glance that made me sorry for asking. "That part's true." The admission came out haltingly, like it pained him to admit it. "A while back, he fell in with the wrong crowd. I caught wind that he was planning a break-in, so I showed up at the house before he could steal anything and talked him out of it. But when we were leaving, the sheriff arrived. He and Jason arrested us, while Levi's partners in crime got away."

"But you did nothing wrong."

"We tried to tell them that. The situation didn't look great, though." Max's chin dipped to his chest. "The homeowners knew me and believed my side of the story. Since nothing was missing, they didn't press charges, but the sheriff and Jason have had it in for me ever since."

"That's awful," I said, knowing what it was like to be on the sheriff's bad side.

I recalled the tense interactions I'd witnessed between Jason and Max since my return. Was the break-in the source of their animosity? Or did it go back further, and the breaking and entering was just the fin of a much bigger fish?

"After that night," he continued, "I offered Levi odd jobs to keep him out of trouble and put money in his pocket. He's turned his life around. I can't see him throwing it away for any supposed loyalty to Truce."

He stopped in front of the noisy building. The slanted light pouring from the windows deepened his worry lines. This was about so much more than his employee or his business's reputation. This was about a friend.

"I believe you," I said. "When we find him, hopefully, he can clear up this whole mess so we can find the real culprit." Determined to find answers, I reached for the door handle.

Max placed a hand on my forearm, stopping me. "It's better if I go in alone. Technically, we're not allowed to invite guests here. And if any of the staff knows about the deck, they'll be more willing to open up if I'm alone."

"Good point. I'll wait here." However, I didn't care for the idea of hanging out with a wolf—dead or otherwise.

When he opened the door, lively conversations and the bouncing of ping-pong balls filtered out. Once he'd disappeared inside and the door shut behind him, the solitude of the staff's cozy village pressed in on me. The all-too-real-looking wolf stalking me didn't help either. While I knew he couldn't hurt me, primitive instinct was hard to ignore.

I tugged nervously on one of my curls as I watched the animal, waiting for it to attack. Instead, it perked its ears and sat on its haunches—putting the fact "it" was a "he" on display. Once or twice, I caught his eye, which earned me a tail wag. Despite his good behavior, I remained motionless until Max emerged from the building again.

Dragging my focus away from the wolf, I faced him. "Any luck?"

He shook his head. "No one has seen Levi. Word got around about the deck, but if anyone knows what happened, they're not saying." He rubbed a palm over his smooth jaw as he considered our next move. "It's late for him to still be working, but I was pretty hard on him earlier today, so maybe he's finishing odd jobs around the resort to make up for things."

"We can ask the front desk if they've seen him," I suggested.

"Yeah. Sure." He sounded defeated or perhaps guilty about their last interaction.

After returning to the parking lot, we headed for the main lodge. We were halfway there when the phantom wolf leaped into my path, cutting me off. Before I passed through him, I skidded to a halt. Although it wouldn't hurt either of us, being chilled to the bone was never fun. I was already cold enough.

The creature's blue eyes locked with mine, then it trotted toward the marina. He paused and turned back as if waiting for me. Did he know something we didn't?

Max walked ahead a few paces until he noticed I wasn't with him. "Vi? Everything okay?"

"I was just thinking. Why don't we check the marina? Levi could be hanging out on your boat."

His lips pulled to the side. "That seems out of character for him. He's not much for water. In fact, every time we go to town, he always finds an excuse to haul something back and forth with his pickup so he doesn't have to sail with me. I've never called him out on it, but I'm certain he's afraid of water."

Wanting to accept the explanation and move on, I observed the ghost again. The beast opened its jaws, displaying sharp teeth before snapping his mouth shut again. I didn't need to hear him to understand he was barking.

I swallowed hard. "We should still check it out."

With a tilt of his head, Max relented, and we moved in that direction. I didn't take my eyes off the phantom wolf, but there was no need to worry about losing him; he paused every few steps to make sure we followed. Once we hit the wooden walkway to the marina, he stopped, shifting anxiously from paw to paw. I guessed a fear of water was something both human and animal spirits had in common. It made me wonder about fish ghosts.

The closer we got to Max's boat, the more my skin crawled. I jumped at every wave that splashed against the dock posts, and my body juddered with each creak of the wooden boards.

When we arrived at the *Crescent,* I noticed something strange about the water beside it. Moonlight reflected off the dancing surface, right down to the tiniest ripples, all except for a dark patch. As I stared, a shape took form.

Already on the boat, Max held out a hand to help me. "You coming aboard?"

I wanted to say "yes" and hightail it out of there. But like it had a will of its own, my hand rose to point a shaking finger. "There's something in the water. I need more light."

He pulled out his phone, shining it around. I just knew

whatever we were about to find wouldn't be good. I wanted to take his phone and look for myself to save him from having to witness it. But I couldn't move.

The beam of light fell on the dark shape, highlighting blue coveralls. I hoped they were empty, laundry that had blown into the water and floated ashore. Then the light caught a pair of sightless eyes.

I gasped.

"Levi!" Max yelled.

He dropped to his knees and reached for his friend. After a stunned moment of watching him struggle, I snapped into action and helped him haul Levi onto the dock.

Saltwater splashed over us, soaking through my thin dress. I was too numb to even shiver. Max shoved aside Levi's damp hair to check for a pulse then linked his hands over his friend's chest.

I had a feeling CPR wouldn't help him—no, a lack of feeling. There was no spirit left. At least, not anywhere nearby. Not to mention, the body showed signs it had spent too much time in the water. Signs I didn't want to dwell on.

"Max, stop." My voice came out strangled from the shock coiling around me.

"Go call an ambulance." His growl echoed across the water.

I crouched beside him, keeping my voice low, almost reverent. "It's better if we leave him until the sheriff gets here."

"What are you talking about?" He wheeled on me. "We need to help Levi *now*."

My heart ached for him. He didn't realize—or perhaps didn't want to admit—his friend was dead.

Placing my palms on either side of his face, I held his gaze. "Max, he's gone."

His eyebrows drew up as though he were silently begging me to take the words back. Not knowing what else to do, I wrapped my arms around him. He hugged me back, hesitant at first. Gradually, his embrace tightened until I couldn't breathe, but I held on anyway.

I wasn't sure how long we remained that way or when I started to tremble. Silence enveloped us, blocking out the rest of the world, like we existed in a timeless bubble. Maybe that was why I didn't notice a boat approach until a beam of light engulfed our faces, searing into my retinas.

"Violet? Max?" a gravelly voice inquired. "What are you two doing out here?"

I recognized Sheriff Reed's voice even before he lowered his flashlight to glower at the two of us. Half-soaked and frazzled, I could only imagine how we looked. Then, his beam paused on the body behind us.

"The two of you stay right where you are."

CHAPTER SIX

The sheriff and his deputy wasted no time parking their boat and dragging Max and me closer to shore for questioning. It felt all too familiar. Whether it was finding dead bodies or seeing ghosts, my magic drew me to death. I'd hoped a weekend away would give me a break from all that, but I supposed it was my witchy burden to bear.

While Deputy Jason Swan interviewed me, Max talked with the sheriff farther down the boathouse, out of earshot. Shoulders hunched, fists shoved deep into his pockets, he looked the very picture of misery, and all I wanted to do was comfort him.

I couldn't imagine how he was holding up after finding his friend like that, under such strange circumstances. If Levi had made a habit of avoiding water, how did he drown? Did someone else do this to him, or was it an accident? And why had he ended up next to Max's boat?

Finally, Jason stopped the recording on his phone and tucked it away, maybe realizing I'd had enough questions for one night. His expression softened the second he switched from his official role to regular old Jason.

"Vi, I can see your brain going a million miles a minute.

I'm telling you this as a friend. For once, stay out of the investigation. A body showing up the same night as the deck collapsing is no coincidence. I don't want you getting hurt." He dipped his head into my line of sight. "Most importantly, keep your distance from Max."

"What? Why?" I gaped at him. "You don't think he killed Levi, do you? They were friends."

He held up his hands. "Look, before you jump down my throat, you've been away for a long time—"

"Not long enough to make Max a murderer. What would his motive be?"

He shrugged his broad shoulders as though it didn't much matter. "Hard to say, but it wouldn't be the first time these two have gotten into trouble. And you found the body next to his boat," he said like the connection was obvious.

"Levi could have washed in from anywhere, carried by the currents. Or someone might have planted his body there."

His chiseled features remained impassive. Clearly, my argument was far from compelling. Either that, or he'd already made up his mind.

While I had to admit Levi winding up next to the *Crescent* didn't look great, I got the impression I could argue perfect logic until my face turned blue and it wouldn't convince Jason. He definitely had it in for the guy. I recalled Max's tale about the B and E, how he'd been in the wrong place at the wrong time. Once again, he was being falsely accused. I couldn't stand the idea of it happening again.

"Max had nothing to do with this," I said. "Maybe he's been down on his luck since I've been gone, but he's not a killer."

"We'll see," Jason said vaguely. "You're my friend, and I'm just trying to protect you from getting mixed up with the wrong people. You don't know Max as well as you think you do."

The words stung, mostly because they rang true. I didn't

know Max, not like I used to. However, that didn't change my belief in his innocence.

I crossed my arms. "You and Max used to be friends in high school. You should have more compassion for him."

He snorted. "Max and I got along when I ran in your circle, but we were never friends. Honestly, it irritated me how close you two were. That scumbag doesn't deserve you in his life." He eyeballed Max's suit jacket keeping me warm.

So was this a jealousy thing? Jason's crush on me in high school had been no secret, but he couldn't harbor lingering feelings after all these years, could he?

When the sheriff's boots thudded on the planks toward us, I reluctantly dropped the argument and faced him. Max hung back, outside the glow of the boathouse's lights, as if to avoid more attention. His focus drifted to the tarp shining in the moon's cool light at the end of the farthest dock, where his friend's body lay hidden. The wave of grief that washed over his face seemed so private I had to look away.

Reed drew closer, his frosty blue eyes scraping over me as though he had X-ray vision to see through lies. Surely, he didn't think I had anything to do with Levi's death. No. It was probably just his usual mounting suspicion. After the last murder I'd solved for him, I'd gotten the sense he knew something was off about me. Maybe he didn't fully believe witches lived around him, but he suspected something was up.

After a moment, he turned to Jason. "If you're finished, we'll secure the scene and interview guests inside."

"Sure thing. I'll get supplies from the boat." He gave me a goodbye nod before spinning on his heel and jogging along the docks.

I half expected the sheriff to drill me with a whole new set of questions, partly because Jason was forgetful and partly to torture me. Before he could, I backed away.

"So, are we done with the questioning? Can we go?"

Reed smoothed his mustache, considering the answer long

enough to make me squirm. "All right. You're free to return to your room." Then he addressed Max. "But it might be several hours until we allow you access to your boat again."

Max waved it off. "Fine by me. I don't think I'll be sleeping much tonight, anyway."

The sheriff sucked on his teeth, likely trying to read more into that statement. "While I can't force anyone to remain at the resort, I'll be strongly suggesting everyone stay here until the investigation is complete. And that doubles for the both of you." He pointed at us.

I scowled. "What? Why us? We were trying to save Levi."

He raised a bushy eyebrow. "With most people, I'd believe that, but you have a habit of stumbling on bodies."

Heat flared across my cheeks. Okay, so it was true, but it wasn't like I went looking for them. Well, I supposed we'd technically been looking for Levi. I still didn't appreciate the insinuation, though. "I also have a habit of finding the killers for you."

He wagged a finger at me. "I'm warning you, Woods. Stay out of my investigation."

"You'd be so lucky," I said. "But I guess I should be grateful you didn't arrest Max and me on sight."

His mustache twitched. "There's still time."

With that ominous statement, he tipped his wide-brimmed hat and headed for his boat.

Max eyed the sheriff's retreating back. "Sounds like the sheriff can't wait to connect me to Levi's death and put me behind bars."

"To be fair, I think his comment was more for me than you. You're not the only one on his naughty list."

He huffed a weak laugh. I wished I were joking.

"How are you feeling?" I asked. "About Levi, I mean."

His face crumpled. "I feel terrible for yelling at him earlier. I can't get the image of him floating in the water out of my mind." He shook his head as though trying to physically expel it. Tendrils of dark hair fell in front of his red-rimmed eyes. "Poor Levi. He was here because of me. I just don't understand what happened. Was it an accident? Or…"

"I wish I had an answer for you, but you can't blame yourself."

The grimace on his face said he didn't agree. "I need to find answers. If not for him then for his family."

His look of desperation tugged at my heart. "Max—"

He showed me his palm. "Don't tell me it's too dangerous or to let the sheriff solve the case, because we both know that will never happen." His jaw tightened as if he were bracing for an argument.

"I don't want to stop you. I want to help you," I said. "Look, I've solved a few murders now, and I'm getting pretty good at it."

Tentative hope flickered across his features. "But why? You didn't even know Levi."

While there were still secrets between us, so much I hadn't told him yet, he needed to know I was there for him. No matter what. "I haven't been the best friend in recent years, but I still count you as one, and I don't like seeing you in pain. Plus, if I can help, then it's the right thing to do."

Of course, this was a gross oversimplification. It was more that my heart couldn't bear the thought of him hurting or in trouble. Helping him wasn't a choice. It was a compulsion, etched into me as deeply as the guilt I'd carried for the last five years. Fixing this—fixing us—felt like the only way forward. Not just for us but for Nolan and the answers he deserved.

His eyes softened. "I really appreciate you working with me on this."

"You're not going to tell me it's too dangerous?"

He gave me an appreciative look. "No. I was thinking that if someone is behind this, they'd better watch their back."

I tilted my head toward the main lodge. "Come on. This

might be our only chance to get close to the deck and search for clues."

Max's gaze slid toward the sheriff's boat. "Okay, but we can't get caught. I don't want to give the sheriff any more reason to suspect me of wrongdoing."

"Then we'd better hurry."

As we put the boathouse behind us and made our way around to the rocky beach, I searched for signs of the phantom wolf, but he'd vanished. Had the spirit moved on to the afterlife? Maybe his final act had been to inform us about Levi because he'd considered the resort his territory. Whatever his reason, he'd helped us, and I hoped he was resting in peace now.

When we arrived at the demolished deck and took in its jagged remains, the memory of our close call washed over me. I shuddered to think of how bad things could have been if not for Max.

The beach was still exposed, giving us easy access, but the tide would come in by morning. How much evidence would be washed away? We were really doing the sheriff a favor by poking around—at least, that was what I told myself.

Focusing on our task, I peered around the dark scene. It didn't take long to realize we wouldn't find much, not without using our phones for light, which would tip off the sheriff. I was about to suggest we leave when I spotted a hunched form along the shoreline. No, not hunched. On all fours. Two pointy ears and a flicking tail screamed feline, but this was no house cat. It was a huge lynx.

My limbs turned to stone. This time, I hesitated to warn Max. There were only so many times I could cry wolf—so to speak—before he started to wonder. Instead, I watched the creature paw at the loose rocks on the beach. They didn't so much as clack against each other. It was a spirit.

What's with all the animal ghosts around this place?

I moved closer, and something glinted in the moon's light. Was that what had the cat so transfixed? A shiny object?

It shouldn't have been a surprise. The crystal we hung on the door at Charming Treasures was a never-ending source of entertainment for Zelda. Every time a customer entered the shop, it would spin, sending rainbows—and the familiar— dancing across the floor.

As I approached the lynx, it froze, watching me with steady amber eyes. Baring its sharp teeth at me, it swiped at my leg. I jumped back out of instinct, but all I felt was a cold tingling sensation where it touched.

Ignoring its continued attempts to stop me, I plucked the shiny object from between two rocks. It was a ring.

Before I could brace myself, my powers locked onto one of the souls who'd worn it. A foggy memory forced its way into my mind. It was distant and vague, like recalling a dream upon waking, but it was clear enough that I recognized Levi standing in front of me, alive and well.

It was daytime—I could tell that much—prior to the deck collapsing because we both stood under it. Well, I wasn't. Whoever had been wearing the ring at the time was, and they were jabbing their finger at Levi.

Their heated words were muffled and distorted. Whatever they were saying clearly upset the young man. He scowled and tried to leave, but the mystery person grabbed him by the shirt.

Of course, the image wasn't focused enough to identify details such as long fingernails or scars. But whether it was a man or a woman, they must have been strong because they shoved Levi against the side of the building and held him there.

He fought back, and they exchanged a few punches before falling to the stony beach. The two tussled beneath the deck for a few seconds then… nothing.

Was that when the ring had fallen to the ground? It was like someone had shut off a TV mid-program, and I was dying

—no pun intended—to know the ending. Had I just witnessed Levi's murder?

When reality set in again, Max was staring at me with concern. How long had the ring entranced me? As he searched my face, I was glad for the darkness hiding my shock.

"Are you okay?" he asked.

"Yeah." My voice shook from both the cold and the lingering images. "I found a ring."

I studied the item in my palm. A silver signet ring with a stone inlay. Onyx if I'd had to guess in the dim light. I tried to make out the design carved into the center, perhaps a crest, but it was too dark to tell. I knew one thing, though; it looked like Garrett's ring.

Was it the same one? Had he attacked Levi? But that made no sense; I'd seen him wearing the ring at the party. Unless he'd left when everyone scattered, snuck down to the beach to hide evidence, and lost it before we got there.

Max drew closer and pulled out his phone, cupping his palm around it to hide the glow from anyone who might see. As the screen's light shone on the piece of jewelry, he drew a sharp breath. I shifted my focus to him, but before I could read his expression, he'd wiped it clean.

"Does this look familiar to you?" I asked.

He shook his head. "No."

And I wanted to believe him. I wanted to believe we'd turned a corner and could finally be honest with one another. We'd agreed to solve this case together after all. That took trust and faith. But then his left eyebrow twitched. His tell; he was lying.

"It must belong to a guest," he said. "Seems like a rich-guy thing to wear. I'll turn it in to the lost and found." He held out his hand.

I closed my fingers around the ring. A voice in the back of my mind wanted to point out it might be evidence, but I didn't want to give it up yet. If I had more time, maybe I could coax further information from the soul who'd worn it, particularly their identity.

"That's okay. I'll drop it off at the front desk tomorrow."

Max's lips parted, but he paused, perhaps searching for an argument that wouldn't sound suspicious or as though he didn't trust me. I mentally dared him to try. Eventually, he nodded and dropped his hand.

What was he hiding? Who was he protecting? I wanted to call him out, but clearly, we hadn't regained that level of candor in our relationship yet. Besides, I couldn't judge when I had my own secrets to keep. So I'd let him keep his. For now.

CHAPTER SEVEN

After a short and fitful sleep, I woke when the early-morning light crept into the cabin. Alice snored softly in the queen bed next to mine. I turned over and tried to squeeze more sleep out of the night, but my eyes wouldn't stay closed. They kept finding the mysterious signet ring on the bedside table. Eventually, I gave in and picked it up to have a closer look.

The inlaid stone was definitely onyx. The design carved into it wasn't a crest like I'd first thought but a wolf's head. As I ran my thumb over it, the same vision I'd witnessed the night before presented itself to me.

This time, I was prepared and mentally pushed it away, a skill I was getting more adept at. I didn't want to start my day off with witnessing what may have been Levi's last moments alive. What I needed was to uncover the owner's identity, and in doing so, possibly the killer's as well.

While I'd been happy to take a break from magic lessons with Helen, I actually wished she were here for a lesson now. However, I doubted it would be useful for the current situation. She was a stickler for the basics, and I was still in magical kindergarten, studying fairy tales about mermaids, vampires, and shifters—oh, my! I supposed most witches learned about their powers at a young age, and I was a late bloomer, but surely, there was an accelerated course for twenty-seven-year-old newbies.

I glanced over at Alice, wondering if she'd have any tips. But her magic was different from mine, more intuitive. Her sole concern was controlling her emotions while baking. Not only did I have to wrangle my own feelings, I had to battle the forces of the spirits attached to whatever jewelry I was working with. Baking had also been a part of Alice's life since she could hold a spatula. I, on the other hand, had spent five years in Europe, running away from my "special talents."

Sitting in bed, I crossed my legs like I was preparing to meditate and focused on the ring. I imagined it was a present to be opened and used my will to mentally peel away the wrapping paper. Working at the corners of the box, I tried to pop it open and search inside, but it remained firmly shut.

Whoever had worn the ring was guarded and secretive. They'd erected tall emotional walls that kept me—and probably everyone in their life—out. If I were a stronger witch, I'd be able to peek over those walls and see into their soul, but not yet. The only memory I had access to was the fight with Levi. Perhaps because, at the time the ring owner let their temper slip, they'd momentarily let their guard slip too.

Giving up, I set aside the ring to try again later, after a strong cup of tea. I pulled on a complimentary robe then tiptoed out into the main sitting area, careful not to wake Alice. The sheriff had kept her late for questioning, and we'd talked for some time before calling it a night, so I knew she'd appreciate the extra sleep.

Just as I was closing the door behind me, a cheerful male voice came from nearby. "Hey, Vi."

A startled sound slipped out of me as I spun and backpedaled into the bedroom door. Heart in my throat, I squinted against the light pouring through the windows that stretched to the peaked roof. No one was there.

As I stepped farther into the room, I finally noticed a faint Nolan lounging in his three-piece suit on the sofa next to the fireplace. He sat in a patch of light that faded his image, which is why I hadn't seen him at first. I groaned in a combination of relief and disappointment. *So much for my paranormal-free weekend.*

Alice whipped open the bedroom door and nearly crashed into me. "What's wrong? I heard you call out. Is there a mouse? It's a mouse, isn't it?" She looked ready to climb onto the dresser.

A sleek black cat leaped onto the sofa. *If there is a mouse, I call dibs.*

Alice yelped at Zelda's sudden appearance. Or maybe it was from "hearing" the cat's voice in her mind, something she still hadn't gotten used to. Unfortunately, I'd grown accustomed to the furball's constant commentary since she'd taken up residence with my dad and me.

She snuck along the back of the sofa, avoiding the icy touch of her former warlock, and perched next to him. Her satisfied expression made me think she'd come simply for the pleasure of annoying me.

Did you miss me? she purred.

I blew out an exasperated breath. "I suppose I should have expected you to follow me too."

"Too?" Alice looked around the room before her eyes widened with understanding. She clutched her robe closed. "Oh… Hi, Nolan. Nice to see you. Well, not *see*, exactly. Er, you know what I mean." A blush crept across her cheeks. "I'm going to go put on something else." She hurried back into the bedroom and shut the door.

Poor Alice was still adjusting to the idea of ghosts, and they made her jumpy. I imagined it was unnerving for her to know they were there but not be able to see them, though I understood better than anyone that seeing them was much worse. If it were possible, I'd have switched powers with her in a heartbeat. Controlling people's emotions through yummy baked goods trumped daily hauntings. In fact, I would have settled for simply being able to bake at all.

I flopped onto one of the overstuffed chairs by the fireplace and faced my fiancé's spirit. "Do you always have to sneak up on me like that?"

He crossed one leg over the other, offering a glimpse of his argyle sock. "What do you want me to do? It's not as if I can wear a bell."

"Fair point," I grumbled, but given how much he loved pranks, I suspected he did his best to scare the pants off me. "What are you guys doing here?"

Since I knew his existence was a lonely one, I tried to hide my irritation. Really, I did.

His bottom lip jutted out, indicating I'd failed. "We didn't want to miss the fun."

"So you hiked all the way through the woods?" I asked doubtfully. While the walk wouldn't have worn Nolan out, Zelda whined about moving from the living room to the kitchen for her meals.

"No. A staff member drove in from town on the forestry road early this morning. We hitched a ride in the back of his pickup."

It was a rust bucket, Zelda griped. *No suspension. My insides are still shaking.*

"You're fine," Nolan told her. "Besides, what else were we going to do this weekend? Mom and Kinsley are shopping in Paris for a wedding dress, and everyone else is here, including my dad."

"So I noticed," I said. This time, I didn't bother to mask my true feelings. Now that the Abernathys weren't going to be my in-laws, I didn't need to pretend I liked his parents. "And not everyone is here. My dad is still at home. You could be keeping him company."

While I'd aimed the suggestion at Zelda, Nolan would have been welcome too. Only, my dad didn't share my ability to see ghosts. In fact, he hated all things magic, which was still a point of contention between us.

The feline heaved a long-suffering sigh. *You're not the only one who needs a vacation, you know. Life has been difficult for me ever since Nolan died.*

Guilt hit me hard in the chest. "You're right. I'm sor—"

I was used to a certain lifestyle with him, she continued. *And now, I've been forced to move into your hovel.*

How was that for gratitude? I massaged my temples. "Fine. I can't tell you where to go, but I don't want to explain to Trent why his brand-new furniture is covered in fur and claw marks. You'll have to find somewhere else to sleep."

How offensive. Her golden eyes narrowed. *I'm not some witless common house pet who can't control herself.*

"Tell that to the gouges in my wooden bed frame at home," I muttered.

Zelda harrumphed and slid off the sofa like oil spilling onto the hardwood floor. *Fine. Cabins aren't really my style, anyway. They must have a presidential suite around here somewhere so I don't have to mingle with you riffraff.*

The bedroom door opened again, and Alice came out in a sweatshirt and jeans. The messy bun on top of her head flopped as she stared down at her phone. "Look. I've got cell service."

"Better hurry and use it before the wind blows it away," I joked. Sort of. The cell service on Charm Island was so notoriously hit and miss that locals liked to make up ridiculous explanations for it.

Alice's forehead creased. "Uh-oh. Lucy didn't waste any time last night."

Curious, I crossed the room to peer over her shoulder. She was on the reporter's personal website, since the local paper didn't even have one. Her latest article's headline read "Holiday Horror: Resort Retreat Turns Deadly."

I cringed. "She already wrote about Levi's death?"

"Yeah. She didn't name him, but it's all in here. I feel bad for his family." Alice scrolled through the long article. "It also covers every unfortunate detail about last night, including the deck collapsing."

Zelda paused on her way to the door—though I had yet to witness how she came and went. *Hold on. Someone died here last night, and I missed all the drama?*

I shot her a look. "It's nothing to be excited about. A man drowned. And it may not have been an accident."

Her fangs flashed. *Even juicier.*

"If you're so interested, why don't you eavesdrop on some conversations? Between a magical cat and a ghost, we're sure to uncover the truth."

Alice dragged her attention away from her phone. "That's a great idea. Speaking of ghosts, have you seen Levi around? Maybe he knows who killed him."

"No sign of him yet," I said. "The only spirits I've encountered are the wolf and that lynx I told you about."

Gnawing on her bottom lip, Alice refocused on the article. "Lucy even threw in her review of the resort for good measure. Poor Trent. He must be so stressed. I wish there was something I could do to help."

"You mentioned baking something for him yesterday. I'd say he needs it now more than ever."

"I think you're right. Some peppy peppermint patties or serenity snickerdoodles should do the trick." As she dreamed up her magical menu, she slipped into her coat and shoes as though it couldn't even wait for a shower. "Wait. You don't mind, do you? I mean, I know we came here for a relaxing weekend."

"That idea flew out the window last night," I said. "Don't worry about me. I've got my own plans."

Nolan leaned forward on the sofa. "What plans?"

Before I could answer, a murmur of voices seeped into the cabin. At such an early hour, I was surprised anyone else was up and about. Through the window, I spied platinum-blond hair passing by our cabin. Teagan.

I cracked open the door and peeked out. Garrett and his two friends were walking along the rocky beach, not from the direction of the main lodge but from the woods. Their hair was windblown, their cheeks flushed, as if returning from an early-morning hike. But the sun was barely up. Had they been traipsing through the forest in the dark?

As I searched for signs of flashlights, the ring on Garrett's finger glinted. So he wasn't the owner of the one I'd recovered from the beach. Then again, it wasn't like the memory had been time stamped. They could have fought days or even weeks ago, giving him plenty of time to buy a replacement.

I pulled away from the door and closed it softly, already knowing where I wanted to start my investigation. I needed to learn more about Garrett and the other Truce residents.

Alice crossed her arms. "You're going to get wrapped up in another investigation, aren't you?"

"Why does everybody keep assuming that?" When no one responded, I sighed. "But yes. I am. Jason and the sheriff suspect Max, and they're either going to arrest the wrong man or waste time while the actual killer gets away."

Nolan combed his fingers through his hair, though it had no effect on the perfectly coiffed style frozen in time. "Why don't you let the sheriff handle this one?"

"Like he handled solving your murder?" I asked, instantly regretting it when he grimaced. "Look, Max is in serious trouble. I'm helping him because he's an old friend. He was yours too. Why aren't you more worried about him?"

"Do you blame me? I'm more concerned about my situation. At least Max is still alive."

I flinched at his unsympathetic response, which was so unlike him. But I held my tongue and tried to be understanding. After all, his extended existence was driven by a singular purpose: to find a resolution surrounding his death. Maybe that single-mindedness was also why he continued to haunt me despite my repeated requests for space while I investigated his murder.

Since I could see him as if he were still with me, it was easy to forget this wasn't my fiancé anymore. This wasn't the man who jumped through hoops to keep the peace and avoid conflict, who drew people together. He was an echo of himself, a reflection of a man rocked by tragedy. A tragedy I had yet to find him closure for.

I sat across from him again. "This is about more than helping Max. He might know something about your death. Your sister told me he was the last person to work on your car before it sent us off that cliff."

Nolan's defiant expression vanished, replaced with a blank stare. "Was he? I… I don't remember that. I wish I recalled more about the time surrounding my death."

"It's okay. I know," I said. "But Max and I haven't been close since the accident, so I can't question him without it coming off like an accusation. I want to smooth things over between us before I broach the subject. It's the reason I came here with Alice."

Alice nodded eagerly, backing me up, even though she could only hear my half of the conversation.

Okay, so I'd come for more than answers, but he seemed touchy about Max, so I felt a partial truth was best for now. "While I don't think he had anything to do with the car accident, he may know something. But it doesn't feel right to get into all that now, so soon after his friend died. And I can't ask him about it if he gets arrested for murder, now can I?"

Nolan exhaled forcefully. "No, I guess not."

"So if you want to keep your best friend out of jail and get your answers, why don't you search the resort for other suspects?"

"Okay, fine. I'll keep an ear out. But for the record, I think this is a bad idea."

He always said me getting involved in these things was a bad idea. Sure, he was usually right, but I wished he'd have more faith in me. Whenever I looked back, I saw how much he used to make me question and doubt myself. It made me realize how much I'd grown during my time overseas. Or perhaps it was due to my time away from him. I was capable of more than he thought.

"I'm simply asking a few questions to nudge the investigation along. What could go wrong?"

Zelda's derisive snort sounded like an adorable kitten sneeze—probably not the effect she was going for. *Famous last words.*

CHAPTER EIGHT

When I stepped out of the cabin, I shivered and drew up the hood of my sweatshirt, my hair still damp after a quick shower. The sun hadn't risen high enough to burn off the mist shrouding the inlet. It hung low, obscuring the treetops and muffling my footsteps, which were the only sounds piercing the peaceful morning. It appeared the resort was reluctant to rouse after the late night. I hoped Max would be awake.

Heading for the marina, I kept an eye out to make sure Nolan wasn't following. Although I knew I shouldn't feel guilty about spending time with an old friend—especially since Max and I barely qualified as that anymore—I worried about what he might overhear. To keep him occupied for the time being, I'd asked him to eavesdrop near the staff housing. At least until Max and I dealt with the whale in the room.

While Nolan seemed to have a handle on the whole ghost thing, including the intense emotions and fixations that came with it, I didn't want to test his limits. How would he react if he learned about the moment Max and I had shared the night before the wedding? Part of me was fearful that if pushed too far, he'd revert to how he'd been when I left the island and start haunting me again. Not in the lost-puppy way he did now but more like something out of a horror flick.

As I came to the spot on the docks where Levi had lain mere hours before, I slowed. The sheriff must have taken him back to town, and the wood had long since dried from his soaked body and our efforts to save him. Still, I skirted the area as I approached the *Crescent.*

When I climbed aboard, I was relieved to find Max seated at the front of the boat, sipping from a steaming cup as he watched the gentle waves roll into the inlet. At the sound of my footsteps, he turned to face me.

There was a subtle shift in his posture, like his tense muscles were melting beneath his flannel shirt. It was such a small thing, and yet it made my heart skip. I'd been worried he'd change his mind about teaming up with me, that during the night, his walls would have come back up. The fact my presence instilled a sense of calm in him gave me hope.

"You're up early," I said.

"I could say the same about you. Here." He held out a second steaming mug. "I saw you coming and thought you might need one."

I took it from him, my fingers tingling from the warmth, and inhaled deeply. Expecting coffee, I was thrilled when I smelled my favorite: chai. "You're still a tea guy?"

"Coffee was never my thing. At least this blend is caffeinated."

As I sat with my back against the cabin, I remembered the times I'd visit him in the marina during my breaks from the store. He'd have a tea ready for me then too. Sometimes, we'd catch up, and other times, we'd simply enjoy a comfortable silence. Looking back now, maybe more was being said in those quiet moments, things that couldn't be spoken out loud because I was with Nolan. How long had Max had feelings for me? And for that matter, when did my feelings for him start to develop?

I brushed the thought away. *Not now, Vi. There's a murder to solve first.*

When I dared to look at him, I was struck by the sadness tugging his features and the dark circles around his eyes. "Didn't sleep well either, huh?"

"I couldn't stop dwelling on… on the case." He rubbed a fist against his creased forehead. "Levi's death couldn't have been an accident. He was so careful around water."

While I wanted to bring up what was really at the heart of his sleeplessness, I sensed he didn't want to focus on his friend's death but on solving the mystery surrounding it. "Is there anyone who might have wanted to hurt him? Maybe someone from Truce?"

"Not that I'm aware of, but… it's complicated."

It was the same line he'd fed me the night before. I moved to sit next to him and nudged his shoulder with mine. "Max, we're on the same team, but I can't help you if you don't open up to me."

"I get that, but I don't know all the ins and outs of Truce anymore. I haven't been back there since shortly after my dad died." His shoulders sagged.

My chest tightened at the reminder of his dad's heart attack six years before. Max clearly still ached from the loss.

I considered the contents of my steaming mug. "Since Truce has been against the resort since day one, do you think Garrett or one of his friends sabotaged the deck? Maybe they wanted to make it appear as though Levi destroyed it and then took his own life out of remorse or something. Garrett was pretty quick to build a case against him after it collapsed."

"I wouldn't put it past Garrett or Shane, but Teagan would never be involved. Levi was her brother. She's always been protective of him. Of anyone she cares about, really. She's loyal to a fault."

At least that explained why she'd reacted so strangely to Garrett's accusation against Levi. He'd been throwing her brother under the bus. But the way Max's tone had softened as he defended her made me wonder if they were friends—or perhaps more. I didn't waste my breath asking, since I was worried the answer would be "It's complicated."

"Let's not forget about Leonard Crab," I said. "The resort threatens his livelihood, so if anyone wants to see this place fail, it's him. He might have sabotaged the deck and Levi caught him in the act, so…" I didn't finish the thought.

Max stared out toward the mouth of the inlet and the sea beyond as he took in the idea. "That's one possibility. The other is that the events are unrelated and we're looking for two criminals. Many of the guests are rich and powerful investors who stand to lose tons of money if this resort falls through. If someone believed Levi was responsible for the deck, they might have tracked him down before we did and things escalated."

I remembered how many of the guests had scattered at the same time we had. If only we knew the time of death. The body had shown signs of how long he'd been in the water, but that was too gruesome to discuss with poor Max. Hopefully, I could get it out of loose-lipped Jason once the autopsy reports came back.

"My money is on Abernathy," I said. "No one has done more to get this project off the ground than he has. Who knows how financially invested he is? Then there's Trent Bass himself." Guilt gnawed at me for even suggesting him. However, I couldn't ignore an obvious suspect just because he was my BFF's crush.

Max sipped from his mug, gaze distant. "True. He has the most to lose. But I've worked with the guy for months and can't see him doing anything like this." He squinted as though trying and failing to imagine it.

"It's still worth questioning him, though," I said. "I should probably handle that. I wouldn't want you stepping on your boss's toes and getting into hot water."

"Thanks." He stood and paced around the deck as if eager

to get on with things. "Could you talk to Leonard too? He won't trust me, since I work for the resort. In the meantime, I'll chat with the other staff and monitor Garrett."

I eyed him. "How do you plan to do that? I didn't think you two were besties."

"I have my ways."

It felt like his "It's complicated" answer, vague and infuriating. Especially since I used to understand him perfectly without us needing to exchange a single word. What exactly were those ways? His wide shoulders and height didn't exactly make him a shoo-in for ninja status.

Before I could press him for more, a rhythmic clicking echoed across the water. I scanned the marina until I saw Abernathy disembarking from his ostentatious yacht. His wingtips landed on the dock with delicate taps, and he adjusted the strap of a black duffel bag slung across his sports coat. As he combed his fingers through his slicked-back hair, he checked his surroundings.

I quickly ducked out of sight, gesturing for Max to do the same. Hunching over, he joined me behind the cabin, and we peered above it to watch Abernathy's progress along the docks. He wasn't dressed for a casual game of tennis, so what was with the bag?

I stood. "I'm going to follow him."

Max grabbed my wrist, his large hand encircling it easily. When his touch lingered, it warmed my body more effectively than the tea had.

"Be careful," he said. "Let's meet at the bar tonight to swap information. I've asked Roxy to keep an ear out, so hopefully, she'll have some information for us."

While I would have preferred to avoid her all weekend, as a bartender, she was in the perfect position to eavesdrop on guests. Also, she had a vested interest in helping Max. Involving her made sense.

"Okay. I'll catch you later." With a last fortifying sip of tea, I set my mug down and scurried after the town's mayor.

Keeping my distance, I snuck along the docks, my footfalls light. When he rounded the other side of the main lodge, I peered around the corner in time to watch him barge through a door with a carved wooden sign that said "Trent Bass."

I waited a beat, wondering if I should keep moving, then voices rumbled out of an open window. The shades were partially drawn, so I ducked low and pressed myself against the building's log facade to listen.

A dull thud from inside made me jump.

"What is this?" Trent demanded.

"What does it look like?" Abernathy replied coolly.

"This isn't how I do business."

"Don't forget all I've done for you." Abernathy's voice was low and menacing. "You owe me. Besides, with the current mess you're in, you'll need all the help you can get."

I yearned to peek through the window, to see what was in that duffel bag for myself, but I didn't dare poke even one red hair into view. My ears were so tuned into what was going on inside the office that I didn't hear footsteps until they scuffed the path a few feet behind me.

"Vi? What are you doing?"

Gasping, I spun to find Alice blinking down at me with those innocent hazel eyes. With a finger to my lips, I waved her closer.

A line formed on her brow before she crouched next to me and lowered her voice. "What's going on?"

"I followed Abernathy here. He gave Trent a duffel bag, and they're arguing about it."

The force of her exhale stirred the dark-brown hair lying across her forehead. "Come on. Leave Trent out of your investigation. He's done nothing wrong."

"He's involved with the mayor. That alone is a mark against him," I whispered. "Abernathy said the bag will help him with the mess he's in. It has to be tied to Levi." Unable to fight my curiosity, I tried to peek above the windowsill.

She grabbed my sleeve and yanked me back down. "Please, Vi. Trent's under enough pressure right now. And I really like him. I'm begging you. Don't make things weird." She turned the full force of her puppy-dog eyes on me.

But I was a dog with a bone. "Someone died, Alice. Don't let your feelings for Trent cloud your judgement."

"Don't let your feelings for Max make you act recklessly," she hissed back. "You're not a detective."

I stared at her. Okay, so I had a habit of getting caught up in these things. And yes, this wasn't the first time I'd interfered in the sheriff's business, but I hadn't seen Alice complaining when that habit had kept her out of jail. I didn't mention it, though. She was still sensitive about the whole fiasco. In fact, it was probably why she wanted to protect Trent, so he wouldn't have to go through what she had.

It was clear she wouldn't be my ally in this case, and I wasn't about to push her. I didn't want to be the friend to show up after a five-year absence just to drag drama into her life. Now that she knew about my powers and why I'd run away all those years ago, any lingering tension between us had eased, almost like I'd never left in the first place. We'd been spending a lot of time together since my return and were in a good place. I wanted to keep it that way.

I sighed. "Okay. I won't ask him about the duffel bag unless it becomes critical to the case."

"Thank you." She beamed at me. "I've gotten to know Trent better lately, and he's a good man. I'm sure there's a perfectly logical explanation."

For her sake, I hoped she was right. But the tightness around her eyes told me she also had her doubts, even if she was too optimistic to voice them.

I was about to respond when the door next to us squeaked

open. Abernathy strode out. Too late to sneak away, I stiffened as he immediately caught sight of me squatting by the window.

He glowered down his long nose. "Miss Woods. Can I help you?"

My mouth dropped open, but no words came out.

Think, Vi! What should I say? I tripped and fell? I'd discovered a four-leaf clover and was picking it for my collection? If that were the case, I wouldn't have been unlucky enough to get caught.

"I was… retying my laces." Thankfully, the shoes I'd slipped on that morning did, in fact, have laces.

His eyes narrowed with distrust, but I wasn't sure he would have believed anything I'd said, even the truth.

Trent appeared behind him in the doorway and glanced from me to Alice. His gaze, though guarded, was much friendlier than the mayor's. "Good morning. Is there something I can help you both with?"

Alice saved me by holding up a plate of cookies I hadn't noticed before. "We come bearing goodies. I thought you could use a break."

A genuine grin transformed Trent's face. "How can I say no to your baking? Come on in." He turned to Abernathy, his expression tinged with finality. "Thanks for the chat. I'll see you later."

Knowing I'd dodged a bullet, I caught Alice's eye and mouthed the words, "Thank you."

Effectively dismissed, Abernathy gave me one last glare before storming off.

Great. Now, he'd be on high alert—not that he ever let his guard down near me, anyway. But this would make it even harder to investigate him. My best chance at figuring out if he had a connection to the murder was through Trent and that duffel bag. So as the entrepreneur held the door open for us to enter his office, I eagerly stepped inside.

CHAPTER NINE

Trent's corner office featured sprawling windows that showcased the beach and the sparkling inlet beyond. But I wasn't there for the view. Instead, my curiosity was drawn by the unassuming closet door, which stood slightly ajar, a black strap sticking out. Trent noticed my interest and casually shoved it inside before firmly shutting the door like he was tidying.

Any other time, it would seem a normal thing to do, but Trent didn't look like his normal self. He wore a misbuttoned cardigan over a rumpled white shirt that nearly matched his pallor. Dark circles ringed his eyes, and a light stubble graced his usually clean-shaven cheeks.

Sure, he might have been out of sorts with everything going on, but with Abernathy involved, I doubted it was that innocent. One thing was certain: I needed a peek inside that closet.

Trent slipped behind his executive desk and gestured to the plaid chairs across from him. "Please, have a seat."

As we settled in, Alice seemed to remember she had a giant plate of snickerdoodles in her hands. Laughing at herself, she slid it onto the desk and nudged it shyly toward him.

"I hope you don't mind," she said. "After last night, I thought you could use a pick-me-up. Please, don't be mad at the staff for letting me use the kitchen. I told them the cookies were for you and bribed them with a batch to share."

"The only thing I mind is you working when you're supposed to be enjoying yourself." His lips twisted into a frown. "Not that anyone is doing much of that right now."

"But I did enjoy myself! Baking is my favorite thing to do, especially when it's for someone I… who appreciates it," she said.

"Well, these look delicious. Thank you." He took his first bite, eyelids closing with pleasure, shoulders lowering a few inches.

I wondered if the reaction was from the simple joy of eating a cookie or the rush of anxiety-soothing magic baked into every morsel. Either way, he looked like he needed it, though it wouldn't eliminate all his woes.

Alice had recently discovered just how powerful her magic was when she accidentally spelled half the town at an engagement party. Since then, instead of learning to grow her powers, she'd been working to limit them, whether it was a hint of happiness in a honey cake after a breakup or a nudge from a focus fritter before a big test. Nothing big. After all, helping people was what she was all about, not altering the course of their lives.

Trent was mid-bite into his second cookie when there was a knock at the door leading to the lobby. As if his backrest were made of nails, he stiffened in his chair again.

"Come in!"

The door opened, and Penelope stuck her head inside. "Sorry to disturb you, but I thought you'd want to see Lucy Litton's article."

He gave us an apologetic smile. "I'm sorry. I'll be right back."

As he stepped away from the desk, the assistant entered

and handed over her tablet. If he seemed this stressed and he hadn't even read the article yet, I doubted the entire plate of cookies would help him once he had.

Alice and I waited as they spoke in hushed tones. Finally, Trent gripped his hair, mussing the dark-blond waves, then thanked Penelope. Instead of leaving, she plopped onto the sofa next to the bank of windows and scrolled on her tablet while she gnawed on her electric-blue fingernails. I imagined there was a lot of damage control to do.

Trent sank into his office chair, gaze distant as though rereading the article in his mind. After a moment, he brushed it aside and refocused on us—or, rather, Alice. "Sorry about that. What were we talking about?"

"We saw the article this morning," Alice admitted. "How are you doing?"

His cheerful act vanished. "Things aren't great. Other media outlets have picked up the story, and it's going viral. But how can I complain? I don't have it as bad as Levi." He shook his head. "Poor guy. I feel terrible that something like this happened here, under my watch."

"No one blames you," she said.

"The investors do." He dragged a palm down his face. "I shouldn't even be thinking about that right now. I mean, a man is dead, and I'm worried about my career. But I've got a lot of people to answer to. Rich, powerful people who are expecting a return on their investment."

I leaned forward, sensing a thread to pull. "And you're worried they won't see it?"

He huffed. "Since day one, this project has seen one setback after another. Missing shipments, animal attacks, malfunctioning equipment. This could be the nail in the resort's…" He petered out as the phrase hit too close to home.

"The fish that broke the net?" I offered one of our local sayings.

"Yes. Thank you." He slumped against his backrest. "If the

sheriff can't solve the case before the grand opening next weekend, I might have to push it back again."

I felt for him. A huge weight sat on his shoulders. However,
that would have given him all the more reason to kill if he'd
believed Levi tried to sabotage his career.

Alice reached across the desk to lay a hand over his, and
the tension around his eyes melted. It was a simple, compas-
sionate gesture, one my kind friend would offer anyone, but it
made me acutely aware of her feelings. I didn't want to ruin
things for her if he proved to be innocent, so I considered alternative suspects.

"You invited Garrett Swift this weekend," I began. "Do you
think he's here to make peace? Or could he have come with
ulterior motives?"

Trent blinked, maybe surprised by the sudden turn in
conversation. "Actually, we had a productive chat last night
about putting limits on hiking trails and boating zones to
protect Truce's privacy. It was the first time he'd agreed to talk
without a picket line between us. I think it went well. Before
the deck collapsed, that is."

"You don't find it strange he waited until now?"

"Not really. He must finally be resigned to the resort opening, knowing there's nothing more he can do to stop it."

Except for endangering guests and possibly killing a man. I
suddenly realized Trent and Alice had a lot in common. They
shared the same optimism and faith in other people. Even for
those who might not deserve it.

"The timing is too convenient, though," I said. "If you
planned on booby-trapping a deck, wouldn't you want to make
yourself seem less suspicious? A friendly chat about burying the
hatchet would be a great way to do that."

He rubbed the scruff on his jaw. "I see your point, but
when the group arrived in the afternoon, Garrett went straight
to his mountain-view room on the fourth floor. He didn't leave
it until it was time to go to the party. The same thing went for

his friends." He turned his palms upward. "The cameras don't lie."

I stiffened. "Cameras?"

"Oh, yes. They're everywhere. I didn't want them ruining the aesthetics of the building, so they're cleverly concealed."

Why hadn't that crossed my mind? Could there be footage of me eavesdropping on his conversation with Abernathy, or worse yet, pocketing a ring from the crime scene?

Arranging my features into a curious expression, I asked, "Do you have any cameras around the deck? Maybe if we review the footage, it will narrow down the suspect list."

His lips pursed as he mulled it over. "I'm not sure that's a good idea. The sheriff's involved, and I want to keep it all aboveboard."

Considering he was in league with Abernathy, exactly how low was that board? Desperation squeezed my chest. This could be a huge break, and I wouldn't take no for an answer.

I laid a hand on Alice's arm. "It's just that we're worried about Max. Since Levi wound up near his boat, they're focusing on him as a person of interest. We only want to help in any way we can."

The frosty glare Alice gave me sent shivers down to my toes. Okay, so I was making her an unwilling co-conspirator in my investigation, but surely, she didn't want to see Max go to jail for something he didn't do. He was her friend too.

Trent's attention flicked from me to Alice, then his hesitation vanished. "You know what? The sheriff already has copies of the footage, so it shouldn't matter. I scanned through them last night, but I wouldn't mind having a closer look myself. Penelope," he called across the room. "You helped the sheriff sort through the videos. Do you mind bringing up the clips you found?"

"Not a problem." She set aside her tablet and scurried across the room.

As she took over his computer, Trent angled the monitor so

Alice and I could see. Soon, a series of shots from around the resort popped up on the screen.

Penelope gestured to them. "As you can see, there's a lot of footage around the deck from when Levi and Max were putting up the required safety signage." She pointed to one clip. "In this one, the inspector arrives to assess the structure. Once he's finished, he and Max move on, and Levi drives away."

I surveyed the collection of videos but didn't ask to watch any since Levi had still been alive then, and the deck had passed the inspection. "So who went down there after they'd finished?"

"The camera only caught one person. Levi." She opened a clip featuring a little red truck and hit Play.

I watched the truck's progress as it drove down to the deck and parked just out of view. "Is there a camera with a better angle?"

"Unfortunately, no."

That was both good and bad news. I wouldn't be going to jail for tampering with evidence, but the footage would be less useful than I'd hoped.

Penelope queued up the next video. "He's down there for a while before we see him drive away again. At least we know he was still alive at that point, though."

She started the recording, and the truck drove out from its hiding place and up to the parking lot. With a few more clicks of the mouse, we were watching the truck from a different angle as it rolled across the lot and out of sight. I noted we never once saw Levi's face.

"How can we be sure it's him?" I asked.

"I guess we can't. That might be important to the case," she said hopefully.

Trent pointed at the clip of Levi parked on the beach. "Except this is all water on the other side of the shot. There's no way to gain access to the area without being recorded, so it couldn't have been anyone but Levi."

I made a noise of agreement but knew that wasn't entirely true. While there were cameras zoomed in tight on the building, there didn't seem to be any coverage of the water. If someone had murder on their itinerary, all they would need to do was swim up, and they'd be out of view.

A detail from the night before came rushing back to me. Leonard Crab said he'd seen Levi hanging around the deck while he was on a kayak. No one would think twice about a small watercraft approaching the shore, and it would be a discreet way to move the body. Maybe Leonard dumped Levi in the marina, either to pin it on someone else or to give the sheriff the runaround, then returned to move the truck.

However, I had to admit, without footage of anyone else around that deck after the inspection, the evidence pointed to Levi being the saboteur. And even if the sheriff didn't pin the murder on Max, his company's reputation would suffer.

"There's definitely no footage of anyone else going down to the deck prior to the party?" I asked.

The corners of Trent's mouth pulled down. "Not the deck, but…"

"But what?" I straightened.

He nodded at Penelope, who brought up the next clip. This one showed the parking lot, where Levi's truck was last seen driving away. A few seconds in, a figure strode into view, heading in the same direction as the truck had gone before eventually disappearing off screen. Max.

"What happens next?" I asked her.

"Unfortunately, Levi parked by the storage sheds next to the boathouse, out of reach of the cameras. We don't see him again," she said in a hushed voice.

Just when I thought it couldn't look any worse for Max. "What about cameras around the marina?"

"There was nothing unusual," she said. "A few guests and

staff coming and going, but no one carrying anything large enough to be… well, a body." She shivered then rubbed her arms.

Trent gave a long exhale. "I'm not sure what to tell you, Violet. I know you were hoping to find evidence to help Max, but the footage suggests he was the last person to see Levi alive."

"But he wasn't," I argued. "He went to search for him but never found him."

He held up his hands. "Hey, I like Max. I don't believe he's guilty. However, when the sheriff reviewed this footage, I don't think he felt the same way."

My mouth opened, ready to spout more arguments, but I realized they were meant for the sheriff—and he wouldn't listen to them. He cared about hard evidence, like the camera footage. And that was incriminating. Hopefully, Max was having better luck finding answers than I was.

Alice squeezed my shoulder. "Max is innocent, so it's only a matter of time before the sheriff finds evidence to prove that."

"Sure," I said, knowing there was a better chance Reed would squeeze into a tutu and pirouette down Dolphin Drive.

Trent raked a hand through his hair again. "Thank you, Penelope."

Taking this as her cue to leave, she gave me a sad smile before disappearing out the door and into the lobby.

Trent released a breath as if he'd been holding it all morning. "I could use some fresh air. Can I interest you both in a tour of the resort?"

Alice jumped to her feet. "Absolutely. We'd love to. Right, Vi?"

"Actually, why don't you two go on without me? I need some time to think."

She gave me a look not unlike Penelope had. "Sure thing. I left a couple of snickerdoodles in our cabin for you."

I thanked her, but I knew I wouldn't eat one. Once I'd

solved Levi's murder, I'd devour a triple batch of her magical remedies. Right now, I needed to stay sharp and keep my mind on the case.

Alice and Trent fell into deep conversation as we headed for the exterior door. I trailed behind, my chest tightening the farther we walked away from the hidden duffel bag, from what might be my one chance at having a peek inside. Trent chuckled at something Alice said, and I decided to take advantage of his distraction.

Making a show of patting my pockets, I clicked my tongue. "Oops. I think I left my cell phone behind. I'll be right back."

In the middle of telling Alice a joke, Trent waved for me to go ahead. Heart galloping, I slipped back inside and beelined it for the closet. A quick glance over my shoulder told me the lovebirds were still lost in each other's eyes, so I yanked open the door.

The black duffel sat on the floor like it contained nothing more than smelly gym clothes. With trembling hands, I unzipped it and peered inside. I inhaled sharply at the pile of bundled bills staring back at me.

Was it a bribe? The timing couldn't be a coincidence. Maybe it was a thank-you for getting rid of poor Levi or hush money because Abernathy had done the deed himself. No matter the reason for the money, it wasn't "aboveboard." Trent was not as innocent as Alice wanted to believe.

CHAPTER TEN

By the time I stepped into the resort's bar, I'd spent the entire day seeking both people and answers but had found neither. Levi's ghost hadn't appeared, Abernathy must have been lying low in his room, Zelda was likely lounging in the presidential suite, and Nolan was still eavesdropping on the staff. Now, as I scanned the classy bar, Max was MIA too. Hopefully, that meant he'd stumbled onto a clue and not trouble.

I passed booths filled with couples huddled together, heads bent close beneath chandeliers formed from twisted branches. If I hadn't known any better, the scene might have been romantic, but the atmosphere oozed tension and uncertainty.

Despite the variety of activities offered around the resort—the property featured a bowling alley, a movie theater, and an indoor swimming pool—the place was packed. But I guessed when the sheriff sequestered you at the site of a potential murder, alcohol eased stress better than a round of ten-pin.

Roxy spotted me from behind the bar, and her shapely lips cinched into a firm line. Not exactly a warm welcome. I was tempted to search for Max elsewhere, but he'd promised to meet me at the bar, and I didn't want to miss him. Besides, since he'd told Roxy about our investigation, maybe she had an update.

As I approached the bar, I wished I'd asked Alice to come with me to act as a buffer. But she was already unhappy with how I'd unwillingly involved her in Trent's office. She'd been looking forward to getting closer to him, and I didn't think investigating him was what she'd had in mind.

A boisterous roar rose from a group of rowdy men using the bar to prop themselves up. I steered away from them, toward an open seat next to a man hunched over a nearly empty glass. He stared despondently into the amber contents. Leonard Crab.

With the resort in so much trouble, I would have expected him to be happy. Or was I observing signs of a guilty conscience?

Taking the free seat next to him, I pointed to his glass. "Can I buy you another drink?"

He eyed me skeptically. "Why?"

"You look like you could use another one. So could I. Who ever thought paradise would turn into a prison? Am I right?"

"Cheers to that." He downed the rest of his drink before gesturing to the bar staff for a refill.

Roxy sauntered over. "What can I get you two?"

Leonard ordered a whisky sour, and I ordered my usual vodka soda, which I planned to nurse; much like the snickerdoodle, I didn't need alcohol affecting my focus. Within minutes, she slid them in front of us, and I told her to put it on my tab. She gave me a curious look but didn't call me out in front of my unwitting suspect.

I raised my drink to Leonard, and he clinked his against mine so hard I worried the glass might shatter. He'd obviously been there a while, and his depth perception was suffering for it.

"Service is great here, isn't it?" he lamented woefully. "And don't get me started on the facilities. I mean, it has a bowling alley. All my hotel has is a weed-choked horseshoe pit stray cats use as a toilet."

I wrinkled my nose then reminded myself to appear sympathetic. "After last night, you don't have much to worry about."

"What do you mean?" He observed me through squinted eyes. Or maybe he was falling asleep.

"The deck collapsing, of course. It would have potential guests questioning the safety of this place. It certainly made me nervous." I twisted a lock of hair around my finger. "I barely made it inside before it fell. And we're not even sure who did it yet. Someone could still be out there setting booby traps."

"Please." He blew out a dismissive puff of air. "Everyone knows it was that maintenance guy, Liam, or whatever."

Tapping my chin, I pretended to think. "Levi? Oh, that's right. You said you saw him in the act."

"You bet I did." He hesitated. "Well, I didn't actually see him do anything to it, but he was under the deck around lunchtime, and he had all those tools with him. So…" He left the unspoken accusation dangling like there was only one obvious conclusion.

"Did you see anybody else with him? Or maybe someone loitering around the marina when you returned your kayak?"

"The kayak?" He peered at me like I was a talking fish before shifting his concentration to his drink. "No. I didn't see anybody."

"You must have come across someone in the boathouse, though," I pressed. "Wasn't there staff around?"

"Yeah. Yeah, of course. That goes without saying."

I noted his temporary omission for later. Sure, his drunken state might have been to blame, but I was certain he was avoiding my gaze. Maybe Max could confirm his story with the staff or check the rental records.

At the thought of him, I surveyed the bar. Where was Max, anyway?

"Wait." Leonard paused, eyes blinking out of sync. "Come to think of it, I did see someone else hanging around the deck."

While he was likely lying to throw me off his trail, he could have been recalling the inspector. Or perhaps my theory about someone skirting the cameras was right. "What did the person look like? Was it a man or a woman?"

"I don't know," he said. "They had their jacket hood up. Not sure why, though. It was a beautiful day. The weather is perfect here. Not the gale-force winds I get at the Shipwreck Shelter. Siren's Call is perfect, perfect, perfect."

Before I could push for more info about the mystery person, a sudden noise escaped him. At first, I thought it was a laugh, but it quickly became clear he was stifling sobs. As he hunched over his drink, the empty glass amplified the sniffling.

"Siren's Call is ruining my life," he wailed. "What am I going to do?"

My mouth hung open as I searched for a response. I felt bad for him. If a big chain jewelry store opened next to Charming Treasures, I wouldn't be too optimistic either.

"Don't forget you have location on your side," I said. "Your hotel appeals to tourists wanting to stay downtown."

"What's appealing about moldy showers, rotting siding, and a roof losing shingles as quickly as I'm losing my hair? Everything's falling apart. Even my marriage. Mandy is leaving and taking little Sammy with her." He wiped his runny nose with the back of his hand. A high-pitched squeal left him, and a line of dribble joined the tear tracks down his face.

I slid him the napkin from under my drink. "Is Sammy your child?"

"He's our dog." He sniffled. "I'm going to lose everything."

"Maybe you don't have to. Trent didn't do all this on his own." I gestured at our surroundings. "He had investors. The mayor wants to increase tourism, and all those visitors won't be able to stay here. This island will need your shipwreck." I cringed at the way it had come out. "You just have to find some investment money for repairs. And... clean out the horseshoe pits."

Leonard sat straighter. Well, except for a slight lean. "You're right. There are tons of people here with money. I should ask them." He slid off the stool as though ready to pitch to the first person he stumbled into.

"Whoa." I held up my palms, partly to stop him and partly in case he lost his balance. "You might want to work on a business plan first."

"Right. Good idea." He leaned over the bar and swiped a stack of napkins before motioning for Roxy to come over. "Excuse me. Do you have a pen I could borrow?"

She grabbed one from next to the register and passed it to him. With a thumbs-up aimed at me, he stumbled to a free table to jot notes on his makeshift paper.

"You cost me my best customer," Roxy joked, but it seemed her narrowed eyes hadn't gotten the punchline. She considered me as she gathered Leonard's empty glass. "So, has the sheriff hired you full time, or are you simply Hope's nosiest resident?"

So much for her Siren's Call hospitality. "I'm looking for answers about last night."

She crossed her arms. "What's it got to do with you?"

I flinched at her hostility. "A man died, and Max is at the top of the suspect list. I'm helping because he's my friend. He said he asked you for help too. You may not like me, but the more minds working to solve this thing, the better. So we should put our differences aside and work together."

"You don't know Max anymore. Not like I do." Her hand fluttered to the necklace he'd given her. "You're not his people. So why don't you go back to your little jewelry store and leave this to Max and me? We've got it under control."

Not his people? What was that supposed to mean? Maybe I hadn't been part of his life for the last five years, but we'd been friends since elementary school. Roxy, on the other hand, had only recently moved to the island. How could she understand him better than I did? Then again, perhaps she and Max had a closer relationship than I knew—and I wasn't sure I wanted to.

Before I could respond, she slapped my bill down in front of me and spun away. I guessed that was my cue to leave.

CHAPTER ELEVEN

Standing on my cabin's porch, I paused to let my vision adjust to the darkness, ears tuned for potential witnesses. But the bar had closed not long after I left, and it seemed everyone had returned to their rooms, leaving the place deserted like a mini ghost town. And I was hunting for one ghost in particular: Levi.

Once I was certain the coast was clear, I made to leave. Then something darted out of the shadows in front of me.

My heart slammed against my ribcage, and I reeled back. As a sleek black shape slinked up the steps, a scream built in my chest.

Zelda purred. *Honey, I'm home.*

The scream left in a quiet grunt of relief, and I willed my pulse to slow. A moment later, Nolan emerged from the woods, hands in his pockets as if he was out for a stroll.

He took in my dark jeans and black leather jacket. "You're dressed like you're looking for trouble."

"Actually, I'm trying to avoid trouble, which is why I'm wearing this, to blend in." Self-conscious, I tugged my jacket closed. "What else am I supposed to wear while sneaking around? A neon jumpsuit?"

"You know there are cameras everywhere, right?"

"Yes, I know that. Now." I rolled my eyes. "I figured if anyone asks, I'll say I'm out for a midnight walk to clear my head."

I wouldn't worry about her getting into trouble around here, Zelda grumbled. *This place is du-u-ull.*

I arched my eyebrows at her. "If you want something to do, you could stop being so stubborn and help me solve Levi's murder."

As though the very idea bored her, she raised a paw to her mouth and groomed herself. *I still don't see what's in it for me.*

"That warm, fuzzy feeling you get when you help a soul in need? Or perhaps the knowledge you've kept an innocent man out of jail?"

When she didn't seem particularly moved, Nolan sniggered. "If you're trying to appeal to her humanity, you should know by now that she's dead inside."

Zelda hissed at him. *A dead joke from you? Those who live in glass coffins…*

"Oh, come on," I said. "You pretend you don't like anyone, but I know you care for Max. Whenever he pets you, you purr like a rocket ship launching."

There are worse people, she admitted, still seeming more interested in her tongue bath.

"If you help, I'll let you sleep in the cabin for the rest of our stay." I held up a finger. "As long as you keep a low profile. I don't want anyone knowing you're here."

All right. She heaved a dramatic sigh. *I overheard the kitchen staff talking about Levi and a lifeguard. A Brandon or a Bennet or something. Apparently, they had a falling out over a bet. Levi owed him fifty bucks.* She waved her tail with a flourish as if to say "ta-da!" *Happy?*

I decided it best not to ask what she was doing in the kitchen. "Interesting, but I doubt someone murdered him over fifty dollars. That intel barely earns you a spot on the front porch. What I need is more crucial. I'm looking for Levi's ghost, and once I find him, we'll need to communicate. Will you search his cabin for a piece of jewelry I can use as a conduit?"

Hmmm. I guess I could do that, but it's definitely sofa-worthy.

I pretended to think hard before relenting. "You have a deal."

Once I'd pointed her toward the staff housing, she slithered off into the night. The smug tilt to her chin made it clear she was proud of her haggling skills.

Nolan took in my outfit again. "I think I'll stick with you. You might need some backup."

I didn't think ghosts made the best bodyguards, but I opted not to point that out. Still, I didn't want him tagging along since I hoped to run into Max. And while the middle of a murder investigation wasn't the best time to rehash old grievances, spending more time with Max had all my confessions fighting to burst out of me. And that couldn't happen in front of my fiancé.

"Actually, could you check into this Brandon or Bennet character Zelda mentioned?"

He frowned. "But you brushed off that lead when Zelda mentioned it. If it's not important, why am I wasting time following it?"

I gave him a wry look. "I wasn't giving up the sofa that easily. Figured she should work for it."

"Touché. I'll see what I can find out." He saluted and headed off into the night.

With that taken care of, I set out on my mission to find Levi, making my way along the beach to my first destination: the deck's remains. While we didn't know exactly where Levi had perished, if the deck was tied to his death, chances were he'd be nearby.

I patted my pocket, where I'd hidden the signet ring from the beach. I wasn't sure how it would help me solve the murder, but I didn't want to leave it sitting around my room. Besides, if I ran out of leads, I could always test my powers by trying to use it as a homing beacon or something. I'd done it once before—though that time, my target had been an animal spirit, which was much easier to track than a human's, let alone one still in a living body. With my pathetic magic skills, it might be just as effective to toss it into the air and accuse whoever it landed on.

When I arrived at the deck, yellow police tape stretched in front of it, though one section was torn. It hung limply, fluttering in the breeze and scraping along the stone. Tingles ran down my spine at the sound. Wondering if that meant it wasn't a "secure" crime scene anymore, I checked if there was anyone nearby. All remained quiet, so I stepped over the tape.

As I moved in for a closer inspection, a shape slithered over the uneven pile of fractured logs and splintered planks. From the way it moved, I guessed it was Zelda trying to scare me again. However, as it drew near, I realized it was much too large.

My body tensed, ready to bolt. Then I recognized the treasure-hunting lynx spirit, and my muscles melted. At least I hoped it was the ghost. It looked so real but for the ethereal glow of moonlight kissing the edges of its fur. Still no sign of Levi, though.

Where is he?

I watched the feline as it sniffed here and there, perhaps from animal instinct, since it had no actual nose to smell with. It stopped next to one of the deck's thick support posts to rub its furry cheek across the broken end. No, not broken, not in the way wood snaps to leave jagged splinters. Instead, it narrowed to a point like a giant pencil.

Curious, I drew closer. The lynx stiffened at my approach. My nerves buzzed at its nearness, but I focused on the divots gouged into the tapered end, all the way to the tip.

Bite marks?

Stones skittered behind me. "What are you doing here?"

Whirling, I found Jason staring me down, fists on his hips. *Busted.*

I pressed a palm to my thudding chest. "I-I'm out for a walk, enjoying the night." My voice sounded an octave higher than usual. "What are you up to?"

He gave me a flat look, like he didn't believe me for a second. I didn't blame him. In fact, I would have lost all faith in his ability to do his job if he had.

"The crime scene is still closed. I'm on guard duty while the sheriff's in town."

I blinked. "Is he already done investigating?"

"Not yet. Cell service is crummy out here, so he went back to talk to the coroner's office about the report."

"So they have the results?" I tried not to sound too eager. "What did they find?"

He crossed his arms. "You were told to stay out of this one. I suppose that's why you're sneaking around. You're searching for clues, aren't you?"

Technically, I'd been seeking a ghost, but information was good too. However, I needed to work on my subtlety if I was going to get any answers out of him. Even a gossip like Jason had his limits.

"Honestly, I thought you were done with the area, since the police tape is down." I gestured to where it lay on the ground.

He raised his gaze skyward. "That was likely Lucy. I caught her poking around earlier, so I sent her back to Hope. No respect," he muttered. "One of these days, I'd love to have a reason to arrest her."

Before he kicked me out of the resort too, I came clean. Partially. "Sorry. My curiosity got the best of me. I'm trying to make sense of what happened last night. I haven't stopped dwelling on it since I stumbled on…"

"It must have been awful for you. While it's not exactly your first body, it doesn't get any easier, does it?"

"Levi. His name was Levi." I hugged myself. "And the worst thing about it is the strange circumstances. I mean, do we have to worry about a murderer, or was the drowning an accident?"

"Drowning?" A furrow formed on his high brow. "He didn't drown. There was no water in his lungs. He died from a blow to the head with a blunt object, probably one of his tools. The coroner believes it was a hammer."

There was the Jason I knew and loved. Now that he was leaking case details like a rusty rowboat, my brain kicked into overdrive. "So it really was a murder? Do you still think it's connected to the deck?" I eyed the log I was studying before. "Those marks on the support posts, they look like—"

"Beaver marks. Yeah, we know. But don't forget, someone intentionally cut the joists. Our working theory is once they saw the damage made by the beavers, they took advantage of it and hoped it would mask the crime." He didn't need to tell me they thought that "someone" was Levi, especially since he'd been the one working in the area.

"The building inspector would have noted the bite marks, though," I said. "So the beaver must have gotten to the deck after his visit. Can they really chew through that much wood in an afternoon?"

Jason bobbed his head. "Beavers can work pretty fast. I've watched them take down a small tree in ten minutes. It would have taken longer to gnaw through these posts, but if they were determined, the time between the inspector's visit and the party would have been enough."

I bit my bottom lip, wondering who would have noticed the damage in that short time frame. Leonard might have seen the beavers at work from his kayak. Then there was the mystery person in the hooded jacket, if Leonard's drunken account was to be trusted. Or pretty much anyone working at the resort, so long as they approached from the water, where the cameras wouldn't have caught them.

"Look, I shouldn't be telling you any of this," Jason said like he was reminding himself. "I want you to understand how serious this is so you'll be more careful. We still don't have the murderer in custody, so it's not a good idea to wander around by yourself at night, dressed all in black." He gestured to my outfit. "And you should especially avoid the marina."

And by that, I knew he meant a certain someone in the marina. "Come on, Jason. Max didn't kill his friend. What about the deck collapsing? You said the two crimes must be connected. Why would Max sabotage the resort that's been paying his bills for months?"

"Maybe Levi rigged the deck himself." He shrugged. "It would put Max's business and reputation on the line. So if he caught Levi in the act…" He let the accusation hang in the air.

I threw my hands up. "You're so obsessed with your personal vendetta against Max you can't see past it long enough to consider any other suspects."

"We also have witnesses who saw them in a heated argument yesterday."

"I was there during their supposed fight," I said. "Max was stressed about getting all the work done before the party, and Levi wasn't keeping up. And he wasn't even yelling. Just frustrated, kind of like I am right now. That doesn't mean I'm going to kill you."

His lips pressed into a firm line. "Are you sure about that? Because you look as if you want to. I'm serious, Violet. Keep your distance from Max."

"Goodnight, Jason."

I spun on my heel then stomped off into the night. Ignoring his advice, I headed straight for the marina to find my friend. I half hoped to stumble upon Levi's ghost near the docks, where we'd found his body, but no such luck.

As I stormed along the wooden walkways, my quiet surroundings amplified my footfalls until they echoed across the water like gunshots. I winced. While I disagreed with almost everything Jason had said, he was right about one thing: a murderer was still out there, and I wasn't doing myself any favors by drawing attention.

Softening my footsteps, I contemplated calling it a night. But as I approached Max's boat, I noticed the cabin's interior light was on. He was home. I'd finally found him.

Relief rushed through my tense muscles as I drew closer to the warm glow spilling from the vessel, closer to safety. The *Crescent* had always felt that way. Or else it was more about who was inside.

Just as I was about to hop aboard, a voice filtered out from an open cabin window, but it wasn't Max's. It was a woman's.

"Fess up already."

My heart shrank in my chest. Was it Roxy? Was I interrupting something private? Maybe running into the murderer would have been preferable. One thing was certain—I didn't want to stick around and hear more.

Slowly, I tiptoed away. Then a male spoke, and his words rooted me to the spot.

"You're going to pay for killing Levi, Max."

CHAPTER TWELVE

Max killed Levi? There was no way.

I was tempted to eavesdrop, but my legs froze with indecision. I didn't want to spy on Max. We were supposed to be on the same team, working together, trusting each other. But what if the fight escalated? He might need backup. Or a witness. Besides, ever since the sunset party, I couldn't shake the feeling there was something he was hiding from me, something that connected him to everything, and I wouldn't accept another "It's complicated" for an answer.

I slipped onto the *Crescent*, crept across the deck, and rounded the cabin nestled into the belly of the boat. A set of closed curtains fluttered in one of the open windows, and I inched closer to hear better.

"How dare you," Max growled. "I had nothing to do with his death."

"Don't lie, Max. Not to me." The woman's voice cracked with emotion. "He was my brother."

Teagan? Since I was sure I'd recognize Garrett's voice, that meant the other man was likely Shane, the Truce leader's other "friend."

Taking a risk, I peered through the slit in the curtains and into the bright cabin. Max was facing my way, but he was scrubbing a hand over his face, so he didn't see me. I leaned closer.

Shane lounged on the built-in bench seat as if he owned the place, close-set eyes trained on Max. Teagan stood rigid, her back to me. The way her arms crossed over her chest was probably supposed to seem menacing, but it looked like she was hugging herself. Despite my unfriendly feelings toward her, a pang of sympathy for her loss trickled through me.

"You can't really believe I'd hurt Levi." Max's voice scraped out as though it pained him to have to say it. "Teagan, it's me."

What did that mean? What was he to her? There was more going on between Max and the Truce group than I'd first thought. What exactly was he keeping from me?

"It doesn't matter what I believe." Teagan's voice snagged like a fishhook. "It's Garrett you should worry about."

"I don't care what he thinks," he shot back. "I looked out for Levi. Before I stepped in, he was going down the wrong path. I thought Truce took care of their own, so where were you all then?"

Shane banged on the table. "Don't talk about things you're not a part of. You haven't been one of us in years."

"So then why are you here?" Max asked coolly.

"Garrett has questions."

"The only questions I need to answer are the sheriff's, and I intend to."

"Is that a threat?" Shane got to his feet and puffed up his chest. "What happens in Truce stays in Truce. You know that. So keep your yap shut before I shut it for you."

Max stepped forward, towering over the man. "I'd like to see you try."

"Enough!" Teagan wedged herself between them and jabbed a finger into Max's chest. "You can't ignore a summons, so are you coming quietly or not?"

He brushed her hand away. "Garrett can't summon me. He might be your leader, but no one controls me."

"If you want to continue living on this island, you have to follow the rules."

Shane snorted. "You mean if he wants to continue living at all."

Max smirked, not taking their threats seriously. "It's a good thing I don't live on the island, then. I live on my boat."

In the blink of an eye, Shane closed the distance between them and drew his fist back.

Whack.

I clamped my lips together to hold back a gasp. Max barely flinched despite the blood welling from a cut on his cheek. Wide-eyed, I waited for him to retaliate, but he actually chuckled.

"You think that will convince me?" he asked. "I could take you both on at the same time, and you know it."

Shane gave him a smug look even as he rubbed his red knuckles. "We have other means to convince you. Maybe we'll pay that bartender bird a visit."

My forehead creased in confusion until I realized he meant Roxy. But why would he call her a bird? Had he been watching too much British television?

"I personally wouldn't mind having a chat with that redhead," Teagan added.

At the realization she meant me, I jerked back in surprise. Between the sudden motion and a poorly timed wave, I banged my elbow against the deck with a loud *thud*.

I froze. Max's focus snapped to the parted curtains. Our eyes met for half a heartbeat, then I drew away and pressed my back against the cabin.

"What was that sound?" Teagan asked.

The floorboards creaked under shifting bodies. The light coming from the window flickered as though someone was peeking through the curtains. A shiver of fear trickled down my spine. I considered diving overboard, but my body felt rooted to the spot.

"Jumpy much?" Max asked with forced casualness—or it seemed that way to me. "It was a fender bumping against the hull."

Footsteps stomped up the stairs, and the cabin door squeaked open. They were coming to investigate.

Max raised his voice. "All right. Calm down before you draw attention to us. I already have the sheriff harassing me. I'll go with you. If only so you'll leave me alone."

The footsteps halted.

Shane's snicker sounded sinister. "Your cooperation is appreciated."

"Lead the way." Max sounded aloof, much like he had earlier, but it was an act. He'd clearly not been willing to meet with Garrett before he had to jump in and protect me. Whatever Max was caught up in, I'd made it so much worse.

My stomach twisted into a French braid. I was supposed to be helping him, not causing him more trouble. And this felt like big trouble. If Garrett's thugs were willing to come to blows and threaten people just to get him to cooperate, what would the leader do once he had him alone?

As the group left, I flattened myself onto the boat's deck. I didn't dare breathe until the sound of their footfalls faded and the loudest thing was the blood rushing in my ears. Then I leaped into action.

Grateful for my dark clothes, I snuck off the *Crescent* and chased after them. I followed them along the docks and back toward the main building, not too close, not too far. I couldn't lose sight of them. While Garrett was staying on the fourth floor, I wasn't certain that was where they'd take Max.

When I was halfway across the parking lot, a voice interrupted my racing thoughts.

What do you think you're doing?

I slapped a hand over my mouth to stop myself from

screaming. However, when I saw who it was, I had a few choice words I wanted to yell.

"Zelda!" I hissed. "Don't sneak up on me like that."

I can't help that I'm better at it than you. At least, I assume you're sneaking around, because you're all hunched over like you have diarrhea cramps.

Ignoring her, I pressed on before I got too far behind the group. I didn't want to miss any part of Max's "conversation" with Garrett.

Zelda didn't take the hint and followed me. *In case you're interested, I checked Levi's cabin. Unfortunately, there's no jewelry of any sort, and I didn't think a dirty sock would help you. He's either a pretty minimalistic guy or the sheriff took everything into evidence already.*

"Okay, thanks for trying," I said dismissively.

So, are you going to tell me what you're up to? Or do you actually have diarrhea?

As we passed the recently repaired police tape barricading the deck, I held a finger against my lips, even though only I could hear her. Thankfully, I didn't run into Jason. It was for the best, since he'd have asked what I was doing and threaten to arrest me for my own good. And he wouldn't have been wrong.

What I was doing was risky, but it was my fault Max was heading off to who knew where. Plus, it had something to do with the investigation, and if he wasn't willing to divulge what he was hiding, then I'd have to find out for myself.

When I hit the main walkway in front of the cabins, I was relieved to spot the trio ahead, illuminated by the solar-powered lights along the path. Keeping my eye on them, I slowed my steps and straightened to look less "crampy" in case someone peered out their window and saw me.

Zelda gave a disgruntled meow. *I'm serious. Where are you going?*

I shushed her. "Two people from Truce are forcing Max to

meet with Garrett. I want to follow them and see what it's about."

That sounds like a ridiculous idea, she said. *I mean, you've had some doozies, but this tops them all. Maybe we should tell Nolan what you're up to first.*

"Don't even think about it. He'll try to talk me out of it. And I don't want to waste time and lose them. Look." I pointed to where the group veered off into the woods. "Where are they going?"

Not sure. But no one knows where you are, so you can't follow them.

"No one knows where Max is either. At least if I shadow them and stay out of sight, I can get help if something happens."

Approaching the forest, I pulled out my phone. No cell service. Still, Zelda was right. I needed to give someone—other than a cat—a heads-up about my plans. When I'd left the cabin, Alice had still been out with Trent. I didn't want her to come back to find me missing, so I typed out a quick message.

> Max is on his way to meet with Garrett. I'm following. Don't wait up.

It was vague enough that she wouldn't organize a search party, but it gave enough info that if I didn't come back, she'd know where to look. I sent it, hoping it would go through if I regained cell service along my journey.

As I switched my phone to silent and tucked it away, something swooped overhead. Was it a bat? I patted my hair nervously.

A branch dipped overhead, and I caught a flash of red in the dark. A cardinal. It perched right where Max had disappeared into the woods, like a trail marker. Or an omen. In one of my lessons with Helen, I'd learned cardinals represented hope and protection. They were a sort of spiritual guide. So I took this as a good sign—for both my current situation and for the fact that I'd finally learned something semi-useful.

As I stepped off the beach and into the forest, my shoes sank into soft moss. I hesitated on the edge of the woods, which were so dense the moon's light couldn't penetrate the canopy.

Zelda's tail flicked anxiously. *For the record, I think this is a bad idea.*

"Then stay here," I said, though I hoped she wouldn't. With her keen vision and sense of smell, she would be my one hope of staying on Max's trail.

And miss you getting into trouble? Never. On the bright side, at least I'll be able to tell someone where to find your body.

And on that cheery note, I plunged into the woods.

CHAPTER THIRTEEN

Snap.

At the sound of a twig breaking, I spun for the umpteenth time and peered at the thick forest around me. The dense canopy allowed only mottled patches of silvery moonlight through, leaving much of my surroundings a mystery as I tailed Garrett's thugs and Max. At least, I was pretty sure I was still on their trail. Not that it mattered if I was about to be eaten by a predator.

My legs threatened to give out as I waited for jaws to sink into my flesh. I saw my life flash before my eyes. Finally, the horrible creature danced out of the underbrush, sniggering to herself. Zelda.

I glared at her, knowing she'd see it with her superior night vision. "That's like the tenth time you've done that," I hissed. "I swear you're doing it on purpose. Keep it down."

You're one to talk. You're about as quiet as a parade. I'm surprised they haven't heard you yet. Or maybe they have, and they're setting a trap for you.

"They'd have to be within earshot for that to happen," I muttered. "I'm afraid we've lost them."

Some spy you make.

I massaged the stitch in my side and scanned the area again, wishing I could take out my phone. However, if my stomping through the woods hadn't already alerted Teagan and Shane to my presence, that surely would. Besides, something told me that even if it were the middle of the day, there'd be nothing to see, no signs of their footsteps in the moss or broken branches to mark their passing. At least, none I'd notice.

"What do we do? Can you follow their scent or something?"

What do I look like, a bloodhound? Zelda, fetch this. Zelda, smell that. You know, we would have kept up if not for you. She turned back the way we'd come—at least, I thought it was the way. *Oh, well. We tried.*

"If I didn't know any better, I'd say you were doing everything in your power to stop me from finding Max. But I'm not about to give up that easily, not when he's still out here. Somewhere."

Fine. Have it your way. You'll be lucky if I don't leave you out here to fend for yourself.

How exactly was she fending for me now? Zelda talked a big game, acting like she would fight off a mountain lion, but I doubted she could handle more than the mice that snuck into the shop. And if it really came down to her being my last line of defense, I wouldn't be able to afford the lifetime of fish she'd demand for her services.

Leaves rustled overhead. Certain I'd lost the others, I risked shining my phone around. A thin tree branch bowed under the weight of something red. Another cardinal. Or was it the same one I'd seen earlier?

Before tucking away my phone, I remembered to check my messages. My text to Alice had gone through during my hike, and I'd received several responses, each one expressing her growing concern. Not that she shouldn't be worried—I was.

Without a coin to flip, I chose a path at random and started forward, only to skid to a stop when a hulking shape emerged ahead.

A yelp escaped me. Zelda hissed and skittered up a tree. I backpedaled into it, wishing I could do the same. The figure closed in, and my wide eyes caught details like fur and a bushy tail. My heart threatened to explode from fear. A wolf.

Zelda's feral snarl morphed into a relieved groan. *Don't worry. It's just a ghost.*

The beast weaved through the underbrush toward me, not a single leaf rustling from its swishing tail. It stopped ten feet away and relaxed onto its haunches as though trying not to frighten me—too little, too late.

As my pulse slowed from a gallop to a canter, I noted its gray coloring and the white encircling its neck. I was certain it was the phantom wolf I'd seen around the resort. Just how many wolf ghosts could there be, anyway?

My gaze locked with the creature's. Was he following me because he thought I'd help him with his wolf problems? While it was sad the poor thing hadn't moved on, I was grateful to run into him. After all, he'd led me to Levi's body, so maybe he'd help me again.

I approached slowly before lowering myself onto one knee. "We were following two men and a woman through the woods, but we lost track of them. Do you know which way they went?"

Silence followed. Not that I could have heard his response, even if it was a "woof." Last time I checked, animals didn't wear jewelry.

Zelda cackled. *You speak wolf now, do you?*

As the canine got to all fours and trotted off, I felt foolish for even trying. Then it stopped and stared me down. It was waiting for me.

I threw the sarcastic cat a satisfied look. "See? He's leading us to Max."

Or straight into his pack's den, she grumbled.

The comment made me trip over my feet. But this was the

right thing to do. For Max. For Levi. Swallowing my fear, I ignored her pessimism and followed the wolf.

Maybe sensing I'd struggle to keep up, it moved at a slower pace. It also cut a path to avoid the undergrowth, and I wondered if that was also a courtesy to me or a lingering habit from life. Like whenever Nolan cleared his throat or when he smelled the air while I was cooking.

As we ascended the mountain range, the nearly full moon rose with us. Its cool light sifted through the treetops that swayed in the breeze, making my surroundings clearer. The woods grew denser the farther we hiked, more ancient and untouched by human beings. Trees twisted around each other, forests growing on top of forests, marking the passage of time. It was both awe-inspiring and spooky.

Finally, our furry escort slowed, and he turned back to me expectantly. Was Max up ahead?

I tiptoed onward, the thick carpet of moss softening my footsteps. Faint noises pierced the silence. At first, it was a cacophony of nonsense, but gradually, my ears picked up on individual sounds: twitters, squeaks, grunts, and growls.

Creeping even closer, I ducked behind a tree and peered around it into a clearing where the moon shone like a spotlight on the scene. I rubbed my eyes, thinking the light was playing tricks on me.

Animals of every kind had gathered together. Birds danced along branches where bobcats lounged. Rabbits hopped next to foxes, and snakes slithered around heavy hooves. However, my attention was drawn to the ones I needed to worry about the most: cougars, bears, and, at the center of it all, wolves.

I gaped at the collection. What natural phenomenon would bring both predators and prey together as if this were a community meeting? Instead of their sights being on one another, a reddish-brown wolf in the center drew their focus. He was enormous, even compared to the two frightening wolves flanking him. This was the leader.

The air in my lungs solidified, and I didn't dare move in case I made a sound. Something told me their ceasefire wouldn't extend to me. But my wolf guide had led me there for a reason, so I wasn't going anywhere. I just had to remain utterly silent.

Snap.

A twig cracked behind me. My heart iced over, and icicles consumed my veins. Every furry head and set of beady eyes in the clearing locked onto me.

Oops, Zelda whispered. *Okay, that time was an accident.*

The scene sprang to life. Birds trilled an alarm, and the smaller animals scurried out of the way as the wolves stalked toward me, hackles raised.

The russet wolf led the charge. As he approached, his lips pulled back into a snarl. Giant incisors flashed in the moonlight, saliva dripping from them as though he were already imagining how I would taste.

I reeled back. My foot caught on a twisted tree root, and I landed hard on the ground. My elbow scraped against something sharp. I barely felt it. I tried to scramble away, but I didn't get far.

With a fierce growl, the wolf charged.

A scream lodged in my throat. All I could do was stare wide-eyed as he came at me. Then my vision went dark.

For a moment, I thought I'd blacked out from sheer terror until I realized it was another wolf darting in front of me. A large black beast. *Great.* They were all joining in the fun.

As it skidded to a stop, its claws digging into the earth, it sprayed moss over me. It faced off with the leader. Snarls tore from the wolves' powerful jaws as they argued over who would get the first bite.

Eventually, the leader backed down. Perhaps because the black wolf was more ferocious and menacing—at least it seemed to be as it turned to me.

I froze, staring at the sharp teeth that would tear the flesh from my bones. I squeezed my eyes shut and waited.

A second passed. Then another.

When I dared to take a peek, the creature had backed off. Not too far, though. Maybe it was protecting its meal from the other animals.

"What do we do?" I whispered to Zelda.

I wouldn't suggest running. Stay calm and try reasoning with them.

Even though I heard her voice in my mind, it somehow struck me as directional. It was coming from above, where she'd skittered to safety on a branch. Some backup she was.

"How am I supposed to reason with them? They're animals."

Goes to show how little you know.

If I could have turned away from the wolf in front of me, I would have shot her a lethal look. Then her words sank in. If they weren't animals, what were they?

It hit me: *humans*. Some of the time, anyway.

Pushing myself to my feet, I watched the black wolf closely. As if to make itself less intimidating, it sat back on its haunches like the phantom had earlier. Well, it hadn't eaten me yet, so perhaps it had been defending me.

I took out my phone and used its light to study my savior more closely. A pair of stormy blue eyes observed me. Familiar eyes I'd been staring into for most of my life.

"M-Max?"

He dipped his black head. It was such a human gesture, not unlike a nod, that a laugh slipped out of me. Or maybe that was the panic threatening to take over.

The phone's light caught his eyes, and they gleamed. It reminded me of our recent interactions, when I'd made him angry—an emotion I invoked a lot lately.

"You're a... werewolf?"

He huffed through his wet nose as though in exasperation. I looked up. The moon wasn't totally full yet—not that I was a werewolf expert. I guessed Helen hadn't gotten to that chapter in the textbook yet.

I took in the plethora of other animals. "No. You're a…" I searched for the word, one I'd learned recently. "Shifter."

Maybe you're not so hopeless, Zelda said from her perch. *Took you long enough.*

"You could have told me," I hurled back.

But there's so much you don't know. Where do I begin?

Despite the situation, the comment stung. I was already dealing with so much, feeling at a disadvantage, and she was rubbing it in? I pushed the frustration aside. There were more important things going on right now.

All the animals stirred. They were leaving, filtering through the trees on the leader's heels. When the clearing was nearly empty, the tension leeched out of my body. This strange nightmare was almost over.

Something nudged my leg. When I looked down, Max was nosing me with his big snout. Instinctively, I flinched. A breathy whimper told me I'd hurt his feelings, but could he blame me?

He headbutted my leg again, more insistently this time.

"What?" I asked him.

He pointed his snout toward the clearing, and I observed the remaining animals. Mostly wolves lingered, along with a couple of bears and a cougar. They were all watching me. Waiting. Did they expect me to follow? My terror returned tenfold.

"Zelda!" I hissed.

When there was no answer, I searched the branch she'd scurried onto. She was gone. I supposed she'd made good on her threat to leave me to fend for myself. Not seeing any other option, I turned and followed the eclectic pack of wild animals.

CHAPTER FOURTEEN

Standing by myself in the middle of an arena, I took in the audience all around me. The torches that lit the tiered seating flashed in a variety of animal eyes, igniting an instinctive fear to run. The human glares weren't much friendlier. I felt hot beneath their stares. The chatter, squeaks, woofs, and grunts blended into one as more and more of the villagers poured in, some in human form, others as animals. It seemed everyone wanted to bear witness, but to what?

Max was nowhere to be seen. The moment we'd broken through the tree line and into Truce, he'd snuck away. Meanwhile, two shifters had led me to a peaked building in the center of the village. It reminded me of an oval yurt but larger and more permanent, with thick logs for walls. I imagined it was a multipurpose space used for weddings, potlucks, sports, and… whatever this was.

As I waited, my phantom friend padded toward me across the dirt floor. Or at least I thought he was a friend. Sure, he'd led me to Max as I'd asked, but to what end? Flattening his ears, he angled his head under my hand. A submissive gesture, or at least a sign he meant no harm. I automatically tried to pet him, and my fingers slipped through, tingling from the frosty sensation.

The ghost made his way to the end of the arena and ascended a raised platform. He sat on his haunches, chest puffed out like he was used to being the center of attention.

His level of awareness struck me. I'd simply assumed he was a clever spirit. Now that I knew about Truce, though, it was clear this was no mere animal ghost but a shifter in their alternative form. Perhaps it was Levi. I wished I could communicate with him somehow and find out, but even if he could understand me, now didn't seem like the best time.

A loud bang made me jump as a set of wooden doors swung open, and a very real wolf loped in. It was the one that had nearly attacked me in the woods. The leader.

He approached the dais before me. However, as he climbed the set of stairs, his furry body morphed, changing shape until his limbs elongated and the fur disappeared beneath tanned skin. When he reached the top step, Garrett was standing fully upright and… er, naked.

An attendant covered him with a cloak made of fur. *Gross.* Since everyone there was some type of animal, it felt perverse, no different from wearing human skins. I wondered if they'd come from past entrées.

The phantom wolf bared his teeth at the leader, muscles tense as though ready to attack. I took it they weren't besties. Maybe we were on the same side after all.

After tying his shoulder-length hair into a ponytail at the nape of his neck, Garrett sat on an ornately carved wooden throne. He regarded me as the audience hushed. It was clear he wanted me to squirm in front of all those people, so I kept my head high and my back straight. Wasn't that what you did when faced with an aggressive animal? Prove you were the bigger threat? Or were you supposed to act dead?

"Violet Woods," he said at last. "You shouldn't be here."

His voice filled the large space easily, thanks to the acoustics and a little showmanship.

"Max shouldn't be here either. But you didn't really give him a choice." I had to raise my voice since I stood thirty feet away from the platform. The performance aspect felt over the top, but my arrival would've impacted the entire village, so I guessed it was fair that everyone overheard our conversation.

Garrett snorted. "Don't make it sound so dramatic. I simply invited him for a friendly chat."

"It didn't look that way from where I was standing."

He smiled like he was humoring a petulant child. "I wouldn't be doing my job if I didn't dig into Levi's murder. I'm the leader of the shifters on this island. It's my responsibility to know everything that goes on with my kind, and no one makes a move without my say-so."

Did he actually care about Levi, or was this part of his show? "And you think Max had something to do with his death?"

"That's between Max and me. It's no concern for an outsider. When I summoned him, I hadn't expected a tagalong. So what do we do with you now that you know our secret?" The question was laced with threat.

I kept my expression cool even as my insides rearranged themselves into a pretzel. "Well, you can't kill me. People will notice I'm missing."

He barked a laugh. "A resort guest who goes on a night hike? People would assume you got lost and starved, fell into a ravine, or that a wolf ate you." He flashed his canines. "A tragedy, but not murder, as far as the public would know, anyway."

I gaped at him, unsure if he was being serious. Then I looked around the building for a friendly face, and when I didn't find one, I searched for an escape route. That was when Max entered through a side door. Shane escorted him like a prison guard, but judging by the determined set of Max's jaw, he wasn't going anywhere.

The phantom wolf got to his feet to greet the newcomer, tail wagging hesitantly. His reaction only reinforced my theory that it was Levi's spirit. When Max neared the center of the arena, Shane shoved him, and he stumbled but righted himself in time to avoid barreling into me. I tried to catch his eye, but he avoided my gaze.

I leaned close. "Where have you been?"

"I knew if they wanted to kill you, they would have done it in that clearing, so I went to find clothes. I didn't want to show up in my birthday suit. This is humiliating enough as it is."

For the first time, I noted that the too-small black T-shirt and sweatpants were not the same outfit he'd been wearing when he disappeared into the woods. At least it was better than a cloak of animal pelts. "I'm sorry I got you into this."

"It's not your fault. I was resisting out of pride, but this meeting was unavoidable." He focused on Garrett and projected his voice. "Violet can't disappear. She has people who would come looking for her."

Garrett scoffed. "They can try."

"Then you risk outsiders coming to Truce."

"It's true," I said. "I sent a text to someone before following Max. Truce will be the first place they tell the sheriff to search."

Garrett's eye twitched with irritation, but he didn't respond.

Max pressed a palm over his heart. "I take full responsibility for her. She won't say a word. I swear it."

"You swear it?" The leader chuckled. "Sorry if I don't take the word of a traitor seriously."

Laughter rippled through the crowd, and Max's jaw tightened. There was that word again. Traitor. I had so many questions. What had gone down between Max and his village? Why didn't he live here anymore?

I thought of Helen, who'd taught me about the existence of shifters. Surely, she knew about Truce or at least had suspicions. "There must be others on this island who are aware of you. What's wrong with one more?"

Garrett considered this. "There are a few outsiders we trust. Then there are those who are part of our world. They wouldn't expose us, fearing their own secret would get out too."

The knot in my chest unfurled as I saw a loophole. There was no helping it; I had to reveal my secret. "I guess it's a good thing I fall into the second category."

He tilted his head with doglike curiosity. "What are you?"

Here goes nothing. "I'm a witch."

The snap of Max's neck was almost audible as he spun to face me. His blue gaze searched mine as if trying to detect a lie. Or was it hurt? The same hurt I'd felt upon discovering his own deception.

Garrett appeared amused by the reaction. "Seems you've both been keeping secrets from one another." His eyes narrowed on me. "How do I know you're telling the truth? Prove you're a witch."

The request brought me up short. I didn't realize there'd be a test. "I-I can't. You'll have to take my word for it unless you can see ghosts."

He drew back as though shrinking away from me. "You're a spirit witch?" Was that fear in his eyes?

"I am."

Uneasy murmurs rose from the crowd. They'd barely reacted when I'd said I was a witch, but it seemed a spirit witch differed from, say, a kitchen or a garden witch. My cheeks heated with embarrassment at my lack of knowledge about my powers. I took a mental note to quiz Helen on it some other time. Assuming I survived this encounter.

"It was actually a spirit who led me to your pack tonight."

The phantom wolf on the platform chose that moment to lift his leg. A translucent stream shot out and landed on Garrett's foot. Of course, it had no effect on reality, but still, who knew ghosts could answer nature's call?

I bit back a smirk. "I don't think he likes you very much."

Garrett shifted uneasily. "Who is the ghost?"

"I'm not sure. He's a wolf, though I suspect he wasn't always."

With some effort, he sat straight again and rearranged his features into an arrogant mask. "Fine. I believe you. So long as you promise to keep our secret, you're free to go, witch. We have pack business to discuss."

His shoulders twitched like he couldn't wait to toss me out like an itchy wool sweater. Either the idea of being stalked by a ghost freaked him out, or he was afraid of me. I decided to take advantage.

"Actually, I'm here about Levi too. I'm guessing he was also a shifter."

Rubbing a knuckle across his bottom lip, Garrett studied me before answering. "Yes. His death shook us all deeply. We're a tight-knit community."

"At the sunset party, you suspected Levi had sabotaged the deck. If you're so tight-knit, then you must know why he did it. As you said, it's your job to know what goes on with your people."

"Tread carefully, Vi," Max muttered so only I could hear.

Ignoring him, I pressed on. "Then again, you also said no one makes a move without your say-so. Does that mean you ordered Levi to do it?"

Garrett's laugh hinted at both amusement and warning. "Why would I do that? Truce has been protesting peacefully. Besides, I wouldn't do anything to draw the sheriff's attention. It's bad enough we've got a spirit witch waltzing in here."

What did that mean? Like I was a bad omen or something?

"Not to mention," he continued, "Trent and I have come to an understanding that will protect this community. We have no reason to quarrel with the resort anymore."

That still didn't mean he hadn't rigged the deck to collapse before coming to their understanding, but I didn't want to waste time quibbling over semantics. This was likely my only chance to catch Garrett on the spot and watch his reactions in real time.

"So are you saying Levi acted without your consent?" I asked.

He turned his palms upward. "We're not even sure he was the guilty party. But he was young and impulsive. I was afraid he would do something like this, even with the threat of punishment."

"How exactly would you punish him? Imprisonment? Banishment?" I left a pointed pause. Perhaps there was something to all the theatrics. "Today, the coroner confirmed Levi's death was a murder. Was that his punishment?"

His features twisted with rage. "Are you accusing me of murdering one of my pack?!" He shot to his feet and barreled down the stairs toward me.

As he closed the distance, Max stepped between us. "Violet's an outsider. She doesn't know how things work here."

He shoved Max out of the way. "You're right. She doesn't belong here!" he roared in my face, spittle flying from his mouth. "Get her out!"

Fear seized my body, and my legs grew weak. Every fiber of my being screamed for me to bolt, but my brain didn't want to leave. With his emotions this raw, maybe I could make him crack.

Before I pressed on, I saw Max subtly shake his head, eyes wide and imploring. I'd never seen him so scared. In fact, I didn't think I'd ever known Max to be scared at all. Slowly, I backed away.

Teagan appeared next to me, breathing hard like she'd been running. "Garrett, we caught the cardinal who followed Violet here."

His nostrils flared as he took a deep, calming breath and finally peeled his focus off me. "Bring the bird in and monitor the witch until we're finished here."

Teagan's chin dipped to her chest in a bow. Then she turned and gestured across the open space, signaling someone. Two men entered, escorting a female dressed in men's clothing a few sizes too big. With the sweatshirt's hood pulled up, her face was obscured, so I didn't recognize her until they shoved her into the center with us. Roxy.

She fixed her gaze forward, head high, as she took her place in front of Garrett's throne. She was a shifter? Apparently, the cardinal who'd been following me through the woods. Shane's comment about the "bartender bird" hadn't been British lingo after all.

So many new questions.

Teagan grabbed my arm and jerked me toward the exit. Before she dragged me off, I glanced back at Max, worried this might be the last time I saw him.

He nodded reassuringly. "I'll be right out. Stay close by."

"Keep moving," Teagan ordered, shoving me through the doors.

I stumbled out into the night, righting myself before I face-planted. She gripped my arm, steering me past an enormous bonfire pit, where villagers warmed their hands and chatted.

Eyes followed me as I marched by. They were filled with curiosity, distrust, and maybe pity for what was about to happen to me. Or that might have been my fear talking. The farther Teagan led me from the center of the activity and the warmth of the flames, the less I worried about Max and the more I worried about what she had in store for me.

Gritting my teeth, I yanked out of her grip. When she tried

to seize me again, I grabbed her wrist. My palm clamped on the series of carved silver bracelets adorning her arms.

A tumult of memories and thoughts hit me. The impressions came too fast for my brain to grasp onto a single one before she slapped my hand away. But it was enough to recognize the familiarity.

She was the owner of the signet ring.

CHAPTER FIFTEEN

Wide-eyed, I studied Teagan in the bonfire light. I recalled holding the signet ring, experiencing her fury and frustration as she assaulted Levi. Had it been his murder I'd witnessed through her memories? Could she have really killed her brother?

She grabbed my wrist again. "Come on. Let's go."

"No way." I dug my heels into the dirt path. "I have a few questions I'd like to ask you."

She threw her head back and laughed, the warm firelight catching the sharp planes on one side of her face, the cool moonlight kissing the other. "You are in no position to question me. You're lucky I don't punish you for talking to Garrett the way you did."

My heart skipped a beat, but I stood straighter and called her bluff. "So why don't you?"

"Because he hasn't ordered me to do it." She looked disappointed. "So you're safe. For now."

"Do you do everything he tells you to do?"

"Of course. I took an oath. And even if I hadn't, it's called respect. Maybe I should teach you what that's all about."

She took a step closer, and that was when I noted her

shapeless black jacket with its sleeves pushed to her elbows. If she'd pulled up the hood, it would be hard to identify her, especially from a distance. I suspected I'd found the mystery person Leonard had spotted near the deck.

"Is that what you were doing with Levi the day he died? Teaching him some respect?"

The sneer fell from her face, and her lashes fluttered. "What?"

"You and Levi got into an argument beneath the deck, and things got physical. Just how physical did it get? Did you kill him?"

Even in the flickering firelight, I saw her face grow even paler. "O-Of course not. He was my brother. I would never hurt him."

"That's not what I saw."

"You were spying on us?"

"Didn't need to." I dug into my pocket and pulled out the ring. "I used this."

Her eyes widened. "You found it."

She tried to snatch it from me, but I stepped out of her reach, closing my fist around it. I shut my eyes and drew forth the memories I'd uncovered the night before. While the ring told me she'd loved Levi, there were other complicated feelings too. Hurt, betrayal, passion, anger.

"You were arguing with Levi, getting in his face," I said, narrating what I was seeing. "He tried to walk away. You shoved him against the building. I can't hear what you said to him, but he seemed afraid of you."

Teagan inhaled sharply. "I don't know how you're doing that, witch, but you can stop it right now." Her snarled words didn't sound so tough when her voice cracked.

I ignored her. "You punched him. Not once but twice. He finally fought back, and you scrambled on the ground."

With a growl, she stomped over and pried the ring out of my hand, severing the connection. It didn't matter, since there wasn't much left to see anyway. Now, it made sense why I'd had trouble extracting information from the ring—and it wasn't only my lack of skill. Teagan was a tough nut to crack.

"What were you fighting about?" I asked.

She scowled. "It's pack business. And none of yours."

It was true. She didn't have to answer me, but I kept speculating, hoping she'd feel compelled to. "The cameras show Levi's truck driving away from the deck, but we never actually see his face. Maybe you killed him, dumped him in the truck, and drove it to the marina to get rid of his body. My question is, why? Did he catch you sabotaging the deck?"

"I didn't kill my brother!" she roared.

Whispers and mutters filtered through the darkness. Teagan cast a look back at the pack members warming by the bonfire. Their uneasy expressions glowed in the darkness like specters.

Gathering herself, Teagan jerked her head toward a spot farther from the fire, signaling I should follow. As she marched in that direction, I lingered behind, reluctant to walk away from witnesses—though I doubted they'd actually intervene if she tried something. But desperate for answers, I followed her across the worn dirt path until grass swished beneath my shoes and the murmurs of onlookers faded.

When we were far enough away, she faced me and lowered her voice. "Levi used to have a knack for getting into trouble, but he turned over a new leaf. We might have had our differences, but I was proud of him for that and grateful to Max for his part in it."

"Then what were you fighting about?"

She pursed her lips. "What's it to you? You didn't even know my brother."

"But Max did. He wants answers for his friend's death. Plus he's a suspect. He could go to jail for a murder he didn't commit. If you're so grateful to Max, then why not repay him by helping?"

Her teeth flashed. They gleamed a brilliant white in the moonlight, matching her hair. "That's rich coming from you. Last time I heard your name on his lips was after you'd abandoned him during the hardest time in his life."

It felt as though she'd punched me in the stomach, and my breath left me in a grunt. But I couldn't argue with her, because it was the awful truth I'd spend the rest of my life trying to make up for. At least that explained why she'd acted as if she knew me at the resort. "Oh, and you're BFFs, are you?"

Her smile widened. "Who do you think was there to pick up the pieces?"

Jealousy flipped inside my stomach like a fish out of water. It wasn't fair for me to feel that way. I'd left him, and he'd found comfort in a fellow pack member. But did it have to be her?

Brushing it aside, I tried one more time. "If you care at all about Max, then you wouldn't want him to go down for your brother's murder."

As she considered me, her fists clenched. Either she was struggling internally or she was thinking of using them on my face. Finally, her hands relaxed, and she stared at the ring in her palm. "This was my great-grandfather's ring. He served as pack leader for thirty-five years. To me, this represents loyalty and duty. Our family has always strived to uphold our ways, so it's an honor to serve Garrett so closely. But Levi was a black mark on our family's legacy."

"Because of his past trouble?"

She shook her head. "Mostly because of Max. Look, I respect the guy, and there was even a time we…" Her harsh features softened before they returned to stone. "But that's ancient history. He's not part of this pack anymore. He walked out on us."

Her tone held such intensity. Was she angry on behalf of her pack, or did she take his abandonment personally?

She shot a quick glance back at the yurt. "Garrett views Max as a traitor, so my brother following in his footsteps—distancing himself from the pack and working for the place threatening our way of life—was a betrayal."

Her assessment seemed over the top, especially since Garrett had said he'd made peace with the resort. Unless his sudden about-face was a lie. Given Teagan's loyalty to the leader, it was pointless asking her. Besides, I had her talking and didn't want her to clam up.

"So you were fighting with Levi about his job with Max?"

"It was a little sibling squabble. Nothing out of the ordinary for us. I wanted to convince him to quit and return to the pack, but he was being stubborn like usual." She wrapped her arms around herself. "No matter what choices he made in life, though, he was still my brother, and I loved him."

Seeing the grief etched on her face, I believed her. However, that didn't mean she hadn't accidentally killed him when trying to "convince" him or murdered him to uphold the family's legacy. Then there was her loyalty to Garrett. If he'd ordered her to make an example out of Levi, would her so-called oath have left her with a choice? Max had said she was loyal to a fault.

Footsteps scuffed the dirt path nearby, and we whirled around. Teagan's fists clenched again, and I shifted my stance—whether to run or fight, I wasn't sure.

Max held up his hands and took a step back. "Whoa. It's me."

At the sight of him, the knot of anxiety behind my ribcage unfurled. "You're okay. Is it over? Is Roxy with you?" I glanced behind him, trying to make out another figure in the moonlight.

"I made sure she got out of the village safely." His wary gaze flicked between Teagan and me. "What have you two been up to?"

Teagan sneered at him. "Someone had to watch your nosy friend."

Apparently, our ceasefire was over. "Turns out Teagan is the owner of the signet ring we found near the deck. But I suspect you already knew that."

He dipped his head, his expression impassive. "I did."

And here I'd hoped for a little sheepishness. The omission had practically been a lie. My chest ached. However, he'd lied about worse, so perhaps my irritation had more to do with who he'd been protecting.

Max turned to Teagan. "I guess that means you can have the ring back."

"W-What?" I sputtered. "It's still evidence."

"The sheriff won't accept it into evidence now that we've tampered with it."

"Wouldn't be the first time," I muttered.

I wanted to argue further. Since it was a family ring, it might have been important to Levi as well, giving me a way to communicate with him. Then again, if he really was the phantom wolf, I wouldn't have been able to hear more than growls and barks, so I let it go.

Teagan eyed Max as she slid the ring onto her thumb, maybe surprised he wasn't siccing the sheriff on her. "Thanks. Are you ready to leave? I'll be escorting you back to the resort."

"I can show myself out of the village, thank you," he said wryly. "But before I go, I'm duty bound to visit one more person. Since I'd be a dead man if I didn't, I hope you won't try to stop me."

A smirk tugged at her lips. "Not even Garrett would. Go ahead." She waved him off. "I'll be watching you, though."

"I don't doubt it."

Moving away from the center of the village, Max led me past log houses of all shapes and sizes nestled among the trees. There were no fences except for those surrounding gardens, and not an ounce of cement or concrete covered the ground. The village was at one with nature.

Max moved confidently through it all, but I stumbled and tripped in the dim moonlight as I reviewed Teagan's confession. Only now did I remember none of the resort's security cameras had caught her going to talk to Levi. However, if she'd slipped past as a wolf, Trent wouldn't have thought to mention wildlife as a potential lead. While it seemed a minor detail, I wished I'd asked. Then, another clue came to mind.

"Max, are there any beaver shifters in Truce?"

"Not for a long time," he said over his shoulder, not slowing down. "They left years ago. Why?"

"It looks like beavers gnawed the deck's support posts. I thought…"

But he didn't seem interested. He picked up his pace as if eager to get out of there. Or else it was more about putting the conversation with Teagan behind him.

Finally, I tugged on his sleeve. "Hold on. Why didn't you tell me who the ring belonged to?"

Sighing, he slowed a little. "Because it would have raised more questions. I knew you wouldn't drop it until you had answers, and they weren't answers I was allowed to give you. So I wanted to confront Teagan on my own."

"Allowed to give me? I thought no one controls you," I said a little bitingly. When he remained silent, I grabbed his arm and pulled him to a stop. "I'm trying to help you. You could have been honest with me."

He studied my face, perhaps trying to remember who I used to be to him—who we used to be. He came to some kind of conclusion and averted his gaze. "It's… complicated."

"I'm getting really tired of that explanation. Teagan said you two had history. Is that what makes it complicated?"

His shoulder lifted in a shrug. "We hung out for a time. It was after you left and has nothing to do with the investigation."

I took that to mean it was none of my business. Which it wasn't, but it didn't lessen the sting of jealousy. "Fair enough."

"Besides, you haven't exactly been up front with me. You're a witch?"

I gave him a withering look. "It's complicated."

We exchanged stares. When neither of us poured our hearts out, Max started walking again. He approached a cabin that appeared older than most, covered in bits of moss and crowded by new trees as though the forest was trying to swallow it. He surveyed it with what seemed like mounting dread before straightening his shoulders and marching up the stone path to the tiny stoop. Reluctantly, I followed.

He knocked on the wooden door with a heavy hand. Muffled footsteps sounded within, filling the silence that had fallen over us. My insides clenched. After watching Max barely bat an eyelash in the face of Garrett's wrath, I wondered who lived there that was so intimidating he couldn't ignore their summons.

With a squeak, the door opened. A short woman with curly salt-and-pepper hair stood on the other side, taking Max in from head to toe. For the first time that night, I felt relief.

Max smiled wanly. "Hi, Mom."

CHAPTER SIXTEEN

Anita Nicolas stepped onto the cabin's porch, wafting the scent of baking out of the house. She pulled her towering son in for a hug, awkwardly battling their height difference to wrap her arms around his neck; he'd clearly inherited his size from his father.

"Max, my boy. I heard you were coming to Truce for a visit."

He cocked a dark eyebrow at her. "That's one way of putting it. I wasn't given much choice."

"I'm happy for any excuse to see my son."

"We're fine. Thanks for your concern." He gave her a lopsided grin.

"I wasn't worried. You are your father's son. You can handle yourself." She patted his cheek. "But if I'd known all it took was a couple of goons to drag you back here, I would have hired some a long time ago."

"There's always the holidays."

She peered around him, noticing me for the first time, and nudged her son's bulk aside to hug me. "Violet, so nice to see you again. It's been too long."

For obvious reasons—at least they were now—I'd never been to Max's house, but his mother had been a constant presence during my childhood. She'd driven Max into town for school every day and hadn't missed a single sports event or, eventually, one of the many meetings with the principal when Max got in trouble.

"Nice to see you too, Mrs. Nicolas."

"Please, call me Anita." She waved off my formality. "You must be cold and tired. Come in. I'll make you some tea." She ushered us inside.

The home was small and cozy, warmed by a fire in the stone hearth. Max poked at the glowing embers and set a new log on top before flopping onto one of the plush couches. Resting his head back against the cushion, he looked ready to fall asleep.

Drawn by the comforting scents drifting from the oven, I followed Anita into the kitchen a mere five feet away. "Smells good. But isn't it late to be baking?"

After donning a mitt, she opened the oven and pulled out a baking sheet. "When I heard Max was in town, I knew he'd want some homemade chocolate chip cookies." She began transferring the treats to a cooling rack on the counter while watching me as though she could bake with her eyes closed. "So, what brings you to our little sanctuary?"

Exhaling slowly, I mentally backtracked to where it all began. Had it really been the same night? "When Max took off with Teagan and Shane, I worried he was in trouble, so I followed them into the woods. Turns out I was the one out of my depth."

"I suppose you're aware of our secret now. It must have been a shock."

"It's not the most shocking thing I've ever learned," I said. "Since you'll probably hear about it anyway, I guess I can tell you. I'm a witch."

Maybe I'd expected her to gape at me as Max had or

shrink away like Garrett. Instead, she nodded sagely. "That's not surprising, since your mother was one."

I stared at her. Had everyone except me known about her? Then again, Charm Island was a small world, and the paranormal one was even smaller.

To me, Charlotte Woods was just the woman who'd abandoned Dad and me when I was seven. Only recently had I learned about her witchy heritage and how she'd passed it on to me. As much as I wanted to delve deeper, exploring that painful history was on the back burner until Dad fully healed from his recent injury. But getting a glimpse into Max's world made me wonder how different my life might have been if I'd had the support he did growing up, if I'd had a witch mother who'd taught me about my powers rather than a human father who'd hidden the truth.

"You look exhausted," Anita told me. "Why don't you sit and rest before your journey home? Do you still drink chai?"

"Yes, that would be nice, thank you."

She busied herself with the kettle, and I wandered into the tiny living room. While the couch tempted my sore body, a collection of photos on the fireplace mantel called to me. Photos of Max over the years filled a variety of frames, and I smiled at the smooth face and awkward haircut I remembered from elementary school. But it was the other subject captured in many of the frames that caught my attention. Max's dad, Myles.

I'd only seen him a few times growing up, but the photos matched my memories of him. A grizzled man with a dark beard and wavy hair peppered with silver. His attractive features were reminiscent of his son's, if a little more weathered and furrowed with worry lines.

Taking my time, I perused the miniature shrine to his memory. Among the photographs was an assortment of items —hand-carved wooden wolves, rocks, a pocketknife—but it was a ring that drew my interest. Silver inlaid with an onyx stone and a wolf etched into it, not unlike Garrett's and Teagan's rings. Or rather, her great-grandfather's, a past leader.

I turned to face Max, half expecting him to be asleep. However, his sharp eyes were watching me.

"Your dad was the leader of the village?"

"Yes. A good one." His full lips twitched up at the corners at some memory. "The village loved him."

"So Garrett took over after your dad's heart attack?"

He laughed humorlessly. "My dad didn't die of natural causes. He was murdered."

The news felt like a kick to the chest. *How did I not know this?*

Anita clicked her tongue as she set a tray of cookies and tea on the coffee table. "It wasn't murder. It's our way, and your father understood that."

Despite being ravenous minutes before, I'd suddenly lost my appetite. Ignoring the cookies, I observed both mother and son. "I think I'm missing something. What happened to him?"

Max dug into the snack, looking grateful for the distraction. When he finally spoke, it was to the cookie in his hand instead of me. "Garrett challenged my father for leadership."

"Like in an election?"

"Not quite. In a pack, the leader needs to be the strongest. Not only smarter and wiser but physically superior, so they fought in their wolf forms."

My mind returned to the open arena in the yurt, and I wondered if it had happened in that very spot. I shuddered at the images of violence that came to me. Sure, they were wolves, but they were also human. "That seems so barbaric."

"It is," he said. "It was a brutal battle. Dad fought with every ounce of energy he had. He wouldn't stay down."

Anita perched on the sofa arm. "He was a stubborn man. A personality trait that runs in the family." She looked pointedly at Max.

He relented with a tilt of his head before continuing. "The

winner only needs to display dominance to win. And yet, instead of simply forcing my father to submit, Garrett killed him."

My breath whooshed out, and I pressed a palm to my chest. "I'm so sorry. Is that why you left Truce?"

Still unable to meet my eye, he approached the mantel to survey the photos. "Not right away. I stuck around for a while after. It was hard being here, though, watching Garrett in my father's place, establishing new rules no one agreed with. Limiting interaction with the outside world, frowning on people dating outsiders, preventing kids from attending school in town. It was a difficult time."

The room fell silent, and my guilty conscience filled in the rest, all the things he wasn't saying that had contributed to those difficult times. While I'd been there for him after his father's death, when Nolan died barely a year later, I'd ghosted him myself, a metaphorical death of a friendship. He'd needed my continued support, and I was off avoiding the ghosts of my past—literally.

Anita twisted the hem of her apron. "Things have gotten worse since then. Garrett rules with an iron fist. People aren't exactly loyal to him. It's more that they're afraid."

Her comment brought Levi to mind. He'd been working for the enemy alongside a traitor, so maybe Garrett had put a target on his back. Was that why Teagan had been so desperate to convince him to return to the pack?

I faced Anita, who seemed older in her grief. "Why do you still live here after what Garrett did to your husband?"

Max huffed. "Trust me, I've tried to get her to move into town with me."

"While I don't support Garrett, he allows me to live here out of respect for Myles. I may not be a shifter myself, but where else would I go? This is my home. We had a good life here and raised our son in this village." She gave Max a kind but disapproving look only a mother could pull off. "Even if he no longer comes to visit."

"Can you blame me?" he asked. "This isn't a home. It's my father's grave." He gestured at the mantel.

She tilted her chin defiantly. "Is it wrong to keep his memory alive?"

It was obviously an argument they'd had before, but I knew it was about more than a few photos. The entire village would have felt like Myles's grave. I couldn't imagine what it cost Max to be here, under the watchful eye of the man who'd killed his father. I doubted it would be any better when popping in for a friendly family dinner.

Max rubbed his eyes. Fatigue dragged at his handsome features. "Anyway, over time, things became more tense. One day, I snapped and challenged Garrett."

I gaped at him. "For leadership?"

"Yes, but I didn't want power. I only wanted to prove he shouldn't have it."

"After what he did to your dad, I'm surprised he let you live."

"It was the other way around," he said darkly. "I was the victor."

I stared at him as his words sank in. "Doesn't that mean you're the pack leader?"

Anita's disapproving look returned. "He's supposed to be. Instead, you left an animal like Garrett in charge."

He scowled. "Like I said, I didn't want the job. I couldn't stand to be part of a community who'd been so devoted to my dad one second and bowed before Garrett the next. There was no loyalty. It made me sick. I didn't want to have anything to do with our so-called ways, much less lead those sycophants." He gestured at the door, indicating all those on the other side of it. "They deserved a leader like Garrett. So I left them to it."

Anita marched over to the mantel and snatched up the ring.

"Your father would have wanted you to lead. He would have rested well knowing his pack was in good hands." She thrust it at Max and pressed it against his chest, over his heart. "Did we teach you no respect for our ways? Where is your loyalty to this pack?"

A mixture of anger and pain warred over his features. "Where was the pack's loyalty when Garrett murdered Dad?"

"There's your father's stubbornness coming out."

Still refusing to take the ring, he stepped back. It clattered to the floor and rolled across the worn hardwood.

Instead of picking it up, Max strode across the room. He yanked open the front door but paused to look back over his shoulder. "It's time we get going. Nice seeing you, Mom."

He slipped out into the night, leaving the door cracked open to suggest I should follow. His mother sank onto the sofa and covered her face with her hands. Torn between them, I hesitated. Each of them suffered for their own understandable reasons. It was an impossible situation.

Without thinking, I bent down and picked up the ring. A rush of memories and emotions washed over me, a lifetime of Myles's love for his family. For his pack.

I'd never gotten to know Myles Nicolas, since he'd clearly been busy leading an entire shifter community. However, the dependability and integrity emanating from the ring made me feel like I knew him. I could see why he'd fought Garrett until his final breath; he'd believed it was the right thing to do for everyone. And because so much of him lived on in his son, I was certain Max would have done the same.

With a mental goodbye to the man, I crossed the room and held out the ring to Anita. "Thank you for the hospitality."

She closed my hand around it. "You hold on to it for now. Max will never listen to me, but he listens to you. Maybe you can talk some sense into him."

I swallowed hard, wondering why on earth he'd listen to me after everything. After I'd rejected him, run from him, hidden for years, and returned only to accuse him of murder.

A surge of shame flooded me for having hurt her son. "We haven't talked much in the last five years. We're not really that close anymore."

She patted my back. "Five years doesn't change everything. He trusts you, or you wouldn't be here right now."

Blinking away tears, I hugged her goodbye and left. I hoped she was right.

CHAPTER SEVENTEEN

The return from Truce went by much faster than the way there had. Not only did Max blaze the most efficient trail in his furry form, but it was all downhill. Also, I wasn't worried about keeping a low profile, so I used my phone to light the way. The thing that kept me moving the fastest, however, was the white wolf tailing us.

Max seemed to take no notice of our stalker, so I assumed it was Teagan making good on her promise to escort us. At least I was too focused on not twisting an ankle to dwell on everything I'd learned that night, on the hurt of being kept out of the loop, and the raw memories that being around Max stirred up. The calm surface I'd maintained since starting the investigation was beginning to bulge, and I was afraid of the whale of emotions that threatened to breach it.

When our descent petered off, Max stopped to sniff the base of an ancient cedar tree as wide as a car. I stiffened, worried he was seeking a place to relieve himself. It might have been a natural thing for an animal to do, but it was still Max. Relief flooded me when I caught sight of a pile of fabric shoved beneath one of the tree's roots and realized he'd been looking for his clothes.

He stared at me expectantly. It took me a moment to figure out what he wanted. With a blush, I turned my back to give him some space to change—both species and clothing.

I studied the dark woods, wondering if Teagan was still following us. As though she'd read my mind, a howl pierced the air. It sounded far away. Perhaps we'd reached a border, and it was a final warning. *And stay out!*

Part of me expected to find the phantom wolf trailing behind us, but we hadn't seen him since our meeting with Garrett. I hoped to run into him soon so I could figure out if it was really Levi. Or it might have been an entirely different spirit wanting my help to cross over. Because I didn't have enough going on at the moment.

While I waited, I texted Alice that I was safe and returning with Max. Hopefully, it would go through if we wandered through a patch of decent cell service. Just as I sent it, dirt scuffed behind me.

I spun to face a fully clothed Max walking around the tree's impossibly thick trunk. His shoulders shifted as if uncomfortable in his clothes or maybe his skin. How often did he transform? Was it painful? There was so much I wanted to know.

Eager to leave, I shuffled from foot to foot, but he seemed in no rush. Shoving ferns and underbrush aside, he scoured the forest floor.

"What are you looking for?" I asked.

"My keys." He patted his pockets. "I know I had them with me."

Picking my way over to him, I swept my phone's flashlight around until something glinted among the moss several feet from the tree. "There they are."

He bent to pick them up. "Thanks. My human eyes are a little weaker than my wolf eyes."

The joke fell flat as the reminder of his secret hung between us, and I couldn't ignore it anymore. "Why didn't you tell me?"

"I wasn't allowed to. You were human. As far as I knew, anyway," he added, bitterness clipping his words.

He'd used that word before. "What do you mean 'allowed'?"

He sighed. "It's pack law, and not one I could choose to break. The alpha has control over the rest of us. It keeps us in check, obedient. It's something instinctual for everyone's survival."

"But you went against Garrett when you challenged him for leadership."

"That's because I have the potential to be alpha. Not everyone does. When I chose not to take up the mantle, it meant he was still in control."

As I recalled the heartbreaking tale, I shook my head. "I don't get why you turned your back on the village. It's not like you to ignore something as wrong as… Garrett."

My phone's harsh light emphasized the raw emotion that twisted his features. "Like I said before, it wasn't only Garrett. The entire village, with their weak loyalty, was wrong. They wanted Garrett, so I let them have him." He said it with so much certainty, but the twitch in his left eyebrow told me that deep down, even he didn't believe it.

"Are you sure that's what everyone wanted?" I asked. "You said not all shifters can stand against the alpha, so their reactions might have just been instinct." When he didn't respond, I squeezed his arm. "I get you were hurting and still are, but maybe you're blaming the wrong people."

His jaw tightened, and he looked away. "You don't understand. You're not from Truce."

I winced and let my hand drop to my side. It felt like a painful reminder that I wasn't part of his world. But while there was obviously a lot I didn't know about him, I understood Max at his core, the way I imagined he understood me. In his pain, he'd isolated himself, abandoned his people, and turned them into the enemy. He'd convinced himself he was doing the right thing rather than facing the messier truth. However, I couldn't judge him, since I'd done exactly the same thing when I'd run away from the island.

I felt the weight of his father's ring in my pocket, but it didn't seem the right time to bring it out. "For what it's worth, you would've made a great leader."

"Thanks."

There were still so many questions I wanted to ask, and by the guarded way he kept looking at me, I sensed he had a few of his own. Before either of us found a place to start, a bush rustled nearby.

Whipping my phone's light around, I backpedaled into Max. He positioned himself in front of me. I suddenly wished he'd stayed in wolf form.

Eyes wide, I waited for some dangerous creature to tackle me. A bear. A cougar. Teagan. What sprang out of a nearby bush was even worse.

Zelda.

The air left my lungs with a grunt. "There you are. I was worried something happened to you."

She neared my leg but stopped short of rubbing against it. *You seemed to have things in hand, so I didn't want to get in the way.*

"Really? Did it seem that way?" I asked scathingly. "You left me for dead."

Don't be so dramatic. You were safe with Max. And by the way, I totally knew how to get back to the resort, but I wanted to be here for you when you got back.

"Somehow, I doubt that."

Max eyed the cat, lips twitching with amusement. "We shouldn't hang around here. This forest has ears. Let's get back to the resort."

My cheeks warmed as I realized he was watching me talk to a cat, and I prepared to explain. However, he simply turned and walked on. His cool reaction sparked an epiphany, and I gaped at his retreating back.

I waited until he was out of earshot before lowering my voice to hiss at Zelda. "Can Max hear you?"

When I want him to. But now, you both seem to know about each other, so I can stop playing the double agent.

"Has he always known about you?"

Not only was he Nolan's best friend, he's also paranormal. I had no reason to hide it from him. There was a shrug in her tone, like "No big deal."

Right. Because why should Nolan keep anything from his best friend? Me, on the other hand, the woman he'd been planning to spend the rest of his life with, he'd hid everything from.

That smooth surface bulged a little more, but I kept my lips zipped and plowed after Max before we got left behind.

As we walked in silence, it gave me time to reflect—more like stew. My heart ached, and it wasn't just over Max keeping secrets. Nolan and Zelda had done the same. In fact, they still were. The three people—or, rather, beings—I should have been able to trust had been lying to me about so much for so long.

When the forest spat us out, it was near the end of the inlet. An early blush of light kissed the horizon, allowing me to see without my phone. Since the rocky beach was slippery with seaweed and algae, we picked our way along the tree line. We hadn't gone far when something yellow glowed amid the driftwood at the edge of the beach, fluorescent in the muted twilight.

I pointed it out to Max. "What is that?"

He squinted. "I'll go check it out. Wait here."

After the night I'd had, I didn't want to be alone, but before I could argue, he maneuvered his way down the bluff. When he returned, he was dragging a kayak behind him. He dropped it onto the ground next to me, and the water trapped inside splashed over Zelda.

She hissed and skittered away. *Watch the fur!*

"It's one of the resort's kayaks," Max said. "If I had to

guess, I'd say it was Leonard's. I checked the records. He never brought it back the day Levi was murdered."

"That explains why he acted cagey when I asked him if he saw anyone in the boathouse," I said. "And when I reviewed the resort's security footage yesterday—"

"What?" His head jerked in surprise. "How did you manage that?"

"This isn't my first fishing trip," I said a bit smugly. "Anyway, the only way to gain access to the deck area without being seen is by water. So this kayak might be evidence." I took out my phone again and snapped a few photos of it.

He considered the vessel, maybe trying to—or trying not to—imagine how the crime had gone down. "We'll leave it here and let someone know."

While we carried on, I mulled over the discovery. Leonard had been the first to lay blame after the deck collapsed, and he came off as guiltier for it. However, it was possible he'd dumped the kayak in a petty move to undercut the competition. If that was the case, the guy wasn't doing himself any favors. I hoped he'd smarten up before he played right into the hands of a self-fulfilling prophecy.

The rest of our hike was silent except for Zelda whining most of the way. At last, the lodge came into view, and I heard my bed calling.

Max slowed in front of my cabin. "We should get some sleep, or we won't be much use for the rest of the day."

As he turned to leave, it dawned on me that he'd barely looked at me since we'd left Truce. It hadn't struck me as strange on the hike back, since we were watching our footing. Now, I saw it was purposeful. *He* was avoiding *me?*

I grabbed his arm. "We need to talk first."

He finally met my gaze. "All right. You want to talk? Since you've heard so much about my secrets tonight, shall we start with yours?"

Uh-oh, Zelda sang. *You're in for it now.*

Max's harsh tone made me recoil. I'd been too caught up in my indignation to notice he'd been biting his tongue too. Before I found a response, Nolan raced up to me along the rocky beach. He moved so fast that his form blurred. Since Max was unable to see his best friend's ghost, he focused squarely on me, his expression unyielding.

When Nolan reached me, he paused to catch his nonexistent breath. "Where on earth have you been?" he demanded. "You were the one who wanted my help, remember? And here you are wandering off in the middle of the night without telling me. You know, you're my only hope of moving on. If something happens to you, I'm lost forever."

How was that for sentiment? I didn't think he'd ever said anything so uncaring to me, so I wasn't sure what to say. With both men glowering at me, all the emotions lurking near the surface suddenly broke free like a giant blue whale. And boy, was I ready to make a splash.

I barked a laugh, making them both jump. "Me? That's rich coming from you. When all you've ever done is keep me in the dark and lie to me."

Max stepped back, looking stricken by the venom in my voice. "Vi... I—"

I held up a hand. "Not you, Max. Well, okay, you too. But I'll deal with you in a minute." I wheeled on Nolan again. "I was in Truce, and guess what I discovered. More things you were keeping from me. Things that would have been nice to know before I stumbled into the middle of a wolf pack."

Growing still, Max scanned our surroundings. "Who are you talking to? Is it... a ghost?"

Nolan crossed his arms. "Who would imagine you'd go wandering through the woods in the middle of the night?"

Zelda rolled her eyes. *I tried to warn her.*

I rounded on her. "And you. You led me right into the wolves' den. Literally. Some familiar you are."

Her ears flattened against her head. Thankfully, she had the sense not to remind me she wasn't technically my familiar.

Nolan held up his palms. "I understand why you're mad, but you can't blame me. The whole shifter thing wasn't my secret to tell. It was Max's."

I couldn't believe it. He knew I'd been investigating a death surrounding Truce. My life had been in danger, and he was arguing about being right based on a technicality.

Max fidgeted uncomfortably but said nothing. He probably thought it was best not to interrupt, given the incredulous expression I was aiming at the thin air next to him.

As I gaped at Nolan, he gave me a puppy-dog look. The immature expression was so at odds with the gravity of the situation that our age difference suddenly hit me. Perhaps he was coming off as childish because I'd had five extra years to mature when he hadn't. He was still that twenty-two-year-old. And he always would be.

I took a steadying breath. "With the danger I was in, you should have given me a heads-up. If not about Max, then about Garrett and the others." A surge of familiar disappointment resurfaced. "After everything that's happened, you're still putting your secrets before me."

"Just Max's," Nolan argued. "I told you I was a warlock."

"At the last possible second." I hugged myself to fight both the chill and the exasperation threatening to explode out of me in ways I'd regret.

"That night, I didn't get cold feet because of what you were. It wouldn't have mattered. I had doubts because we were partners who were supposed to tell each other everything. How could I trust you after I found out you'd been hiding the real you for so long? And it seems nothing has changed."

Nolan's mouth opened and closed wordlessly, as though I'd taken my ring off and broken the connection. Before he figured out what to say, I stormed off.

Stones crunched under my feet as I stomped toward the

marina, the one place he wouldn't go. I knew Max would follow. The conversation between us had been five years in the making, and suddenly, I couldn't wait even a few hours to have it.

Finally catching up to me on the docks, he clamped a hand on my shoulder and spun me around to face him. "Violet, who were you talking to?" But judging by the tortured expression on his face, he already knew.

"Nolan."

CHAPTER EIGHTEEN

Max set a cup of tea on the dining table in front of me. Well, it was sometimes a dining table, other times a bed, and probably even made an impromptu ironing board if he ever needed one. Not that he was an ironing kind of guy. But what did I know about the real Max? Not as much as I'd thought, apparently. Though I supposed it was a two-way street.

He surveyed the tiny cabin. "Are we… alone?"

"Yeah," I said. "Ghosts don't like water."

Relaxing a little, he leaned against the galley counter and waited patiently for me to begin. I gathered my thoughts as I blew on my tea, my brain craving the caffeine after the long night hiking through the woods. When he cleared his throat, it was obvious his patience was running thin.

I sighed and set aside the cup. "Nolan was my first ghost. He came to me when I woke in the hospital after the accident."

Max's face hardened like a dam holding back emotions, but he said nothing, waiting for me to continue.

"I didn't know I was a witch back then. I found out when I returned to the island a few months ago. In fact, I refused to admit magic existed, even after Nolan showed me his powers at the rehearsal dinner." I studied the tabletop. "I didn't exactly take the news well."

"So that's why you were upset when you showed up at my boat." He stared out the window, likely lost in thoughts of that night. "Remember how I told you, leading up to the wedding, Nolan and I had been fighting?" He waited for me to nod. "His secret was the reason. I knew he hadn't told you yet, and I couldn't stand by and watch him keep you in the dark any longer. Not when you were going to be married. We had a huge fight at the rehearsal dinner, and I gave him an ultimatum. If he didn't tell you that night, I would."

I recalled seeing Max storm off before the main course had even been served. "Is that why you left the party?"

"I didn't want to ruin the night." His lips twisted into a humorless smile, probably thinking it would have been the least of our worries. "At least Nolan came clean in the end."

"He did," I said. However, now that I knew Max had intervened, I doubted Nolan had ever intended to tell me. "I didn't believe him, though. Of course, it freaked me out at first, but as I ran away, my brain made up excuses for what I saw. Even when Nolan came to me as a ghost, I assumed it was posttraumatic stress or a curse. A punishment."

A wrinkle formed on Max's brow. "Punishment for what?"

"For the accident," I said in a hushed tone. Not willing to wait any longer, I took a sip of scalding tea and swallowed. It went down easier than the confession was coming out. "None of it would have happened if it hadn't been for me."

The wrinkle deepened. "Violet, you can't really think that. You did nothing—"

I held up my palm to stop him. "I've been telling myself that for years, but what my brain tells me and what my heart believes are two different things. If I hadn't run away from the rehearsal dinner, Nolan wouldn't have been driving all over town looking for me."

He opened his mouth as though to argue again, but I waved it away.

"Anyway," I continued, "after his death, he haunted me for days. I wasn't able to communicate with him, of course. I've recently discovered my ability to hear ghosts requires a conduit, a piece of jewelry connected to the person. That's why I wear this." Holding up my hand, I showed him my wedding ring. "Nolan was different back then, haunting me wherever I went. In my room, in the shower, following me all over town. I barely slept. I thought I was losing my mind."

Max took a seat next to me on the built-in bench seat. "I wish I'd known what you were going through."

"So do I. Things might have gone differently if I'd confided in you." I coiled a lock of hair around my finger. "At the time, it felt like the world was against me. Even Nolan's parents blamed me for his death, and they vowed to destroy my family's business. And then there was the sheriff. He suspected me of hiding something about the accident, and I don't blame him. We drove off a cliff and into the bay. How could anyone survive that?"

A lump formed in my throat, and I took another sip of tea. "I now know my survival was thanks to Nolan's protective powers. The part I can't explain was how I got to shore. I remember getting out of my seat belt, the window breaking, and flashes of something or... someone." I narrowed my eyes at Max as my newfound knowledge about his nature reshaped the memories. "It was you, wasn't it? You saved me."

He ducked his head. "Most shifters can only change into one thing, maybe two, but not well. I can change into many animals."

Things clicked into place, and not just from that night. My most recent near miss came to mind. I touched my upper arm, where a freshly healed wound hid, and recalled the feathered friend that had come between me and a pastry chef's knife.

"Can you transform into a hawk?"

He nodded.

"What about the night in the marina when the ferry captain nearly drowned me? I wouldn't have survived if not for the help of… a sea creature?"

He huffed. "A dolphin. I prefer sharks, but I decided against that because of your childhood fear."

"Oh, thanks for that." I wouldn't tell him I'd thought it was a shark anyway.

Ever since I'd returned, I thought Max barely cared anymore, that after my absence, he'd all but given up on me. However, he'd been there all along, looking out for me. He'd never stopped caring.

"So what about the night of the accident?" I asked.

Max stared down at his palms. "After you left my boat with Nolan, I followed his car. I don't know what I planned to do. I really wanted you guys to work things out, but if you didn't… Well, I'd told you how I felt, and I was done pining away as the silent friend."

My nose wrinkled as I sorted through my foggy memories of that night. "I don't remember anyone tailing us."

"I wasn't driving." He fluttered his hands like wings. "Hawk."

"Right. Of course."

"When I saw the car drive off the cliff, it practically tore my heart out. I assumed you were both…" His Adam's apple bobbed. "I flew down to the water's surface as quickly as I could. When I shifted and dove in, I didn't think there'd be anyone to save. I just couldn't stand the idea of the two of you sitting at the bottom of the bay. But when I got to the vehicle, there you were, miraculously alive. I knew Nolan had somehow done that."

Jaw dropping, I stared at him in awe. "I remember you reaching into the car for me, your arms around me. I thought I imagined it because you had a tail."

His cheeks brightened. "I had to swim fast, but I also needed my arms."

Despite the heaviness of the moment, a giggle slipped out. "You were a mermaid?"

"No. I was partially transformed. And I believe the term is merman." He succumbed to a brief chuckle. "Anyway. By the time I swam you to shore, you'd lost consciousness and needed medical attention. I shifted back into human form and carried you up to the road. When headlights approached, I set you on the roadside and hid because… well, for one, I was naked. And two, how would I explain how I got you out of the vehicle? I couldn't risk revealing the pack's secret. So I made myself scarce and watched as Jason spotted you and pulled over."

My body shuddered at the memory of being trapped in the vehicle. Or what had nearly been my casket. "I would have sunk with that car if it hadn't been for you. You saved my life."

He gave me a sad smile. "I can't tell you how relieved I was when I heard you were going to be okay. I tried to visit you at the hospital, but the doctor wouldn't let me."

"Yeah. By that point, I'd seen Nolan, and they had to give me sedatives."

He twisted to face me. "I get why you left now. What I don't understand is why you didn't stay in touch."

I hung my head. And here I'd thought recounting the accident was going to be the hardest part. "Because the longer I was gone, the easier it was to ignore everything and pretend none of it happened. I even ignored the ghosts I continued to see. I thought about calling you a million times, though. That part never got easier."

"Why didn't you?"

"I just…" The boat was suddenly too cramped, too hot. I jumped to my feet and walked the short distance to his bed, putting space between us. "I felt so guilty."

His chin lowered. "Because I told you I loved you."

"No." I pressed a hand over my chest, feeling the irregular

thrum of my heart beneath my palm. "Because I felt the same way."

Spoken aloud for the first time, the words came out in a rush. Even though there was no controlling who I loved, it was like I was betraying Nolan, the man I was supposed to marry, the man who'd sacrificed himself to save me. I felt like the worst person in the world.

Max inhaled sharply but said nothing. I wasn't sure if that was better or if I'd actually hoped he'd say he still loved me. But he didn't, and I didn't know what that meant.

I hurried to fill the silence. "That night, when you asked me to sail away with you, it was all I wanted to do. But I was so confused. Then the accident happened, and Nolan was a ghost, and shame on me for even contemplating being happy without him, moving on when he couldn't. He was still here on our plane, trapped and miserable. So I needed to be miserable too. It was what I deserved."

"That's not true." His voice was thick with emotion. "You deserve to be happy. And I'm sure Nolan wants that for you too."

Biting my lip, I said nothing. In theory, my fiancé would want that. However, Nolan was still understandably stuck in our past. I doubted he would congratulate me on moving on with his best friend. Not that I dared to hope Max was an option anymore.

"Since returning, I've learned my relationship with Nolan wasn't what I thought it was," I said. "I'm also learning neither was yours and mine. I don't know where I stand with anyone right now."

While I hadn't meant it to be hurtful, a wince lanced across his face, and I wished I understood why. Was it regret from our past? Or was it something more current?

"You understand why I didn't tell you, right?" He sounded pained. "Maybe I could have broken through the compulsion once I'd distanced myself from the pack. I should have tried, but I was afraid."

"That Garrett would punish you?"

"No. I was worried about what you'd think of me."

Considering how I'd reacted to Nolan's news, I didn't blame him. "I guess we'll never know."

His gaze dropped from mine, and neither of us could figure out what to say next. Everything that had come between us five years ago and ever since had been laid bare. Maybe all we needed was time to process and come out the other side, perhaps better for it, perhaps worse. Only time would tell.

In the meantime, my mind returned to the promise I'd made to Nolan. He was right to be impatient with me. I'd been taking too long to look into his murder, dragging my feet because I was afraid to face my past. Now that Max and I were finally being open with one another, it was time to put my worries aside and simply ask him if he knew anything.

However, before I could broach the subject, rhythmic footsteps interrupted the silence. They thudded along the dock outside the boat, growing closer.

It seemed our time for dredging up the past was done.

CHAPTER NINETEEN

Knock, knock, knock.

I locked eyes with Max, guilt weighing on me for our clandestine meeting. But who did we have to hide our old feelings from? Well, except for Nolan, and he was too afraid of the water to come out to the *Crescent*. And unable to knock, for that matter.

When Max opened the little cabin door, I squinted against the light silhouetting the early visitor and realized the sun had risen during our talk. When my vision adjusted, Roxy's pretty face came into focus, dark skin golden in the early morning light. Okay, so maybe we needed to feel guilty about her, even if I didn't know the extent of her relationship with Max.

She hesitated at the sight of me but quickly recovered. "Max, Trent has been looking for you. A pipe in Leonard's guest room burst. There's water everywhere."

Leonard again. Something told me it wasn't an accident.

"Okay. I'll see what I can do." He rolled his shoulders as though trying to shift any lingering heaviness from our conversation. "Vi, I'm sorry. Can we finish this another time?"

"Sure. We'll catch up later." I wasn't sure I could talk anymore, anyway. I needed time to mull things over.

Max grabbed his toolbox and disembarked before navigating the marina's pathways at a jog. Roxy and I followed behind at a slower pace. My feet felt heavy after my long night and scuffed the wooden boards as we headed back to the main lodge. If Roxy was tired, she didn't show it, which made me wonder if flying took as much energy as walking. Posture rigid, she snatched glances at me out of the corner of her eye. A thick silence pressed in around us, and I struggled to find small talk to fill it.

"So, I guess you know I'm a shifter," she blurted.

Good old Roxy. I could always count on her for a candid discussion. "Yes. Cardinals are beautiful birds. The red streak in your hair makes sense now."

She absently tugged on the scarlet braid. "It's my own private joke."

"Well, your secret is safe with me. And if it makes you feel any better, I'm a witch." I figured it didn't matter if I told her, since the rest of the shifter community was aware. Maybe it would even help smooth things over between us. I might not have been a fan of her relationship with Max, but I didn't need her as an enemy.

"That's... cool." She studied me with more interest but stayed true to her unruffled nature and said nothing more about it. "Look. I'm sorry for my attitude at the bar last night. I can get protective of the people I care about, and I wasn't sure I could trust you."

"Do you trust me now?"

She pulled her lips to the side as she considered it. "I trust you have Max's best interests at heart."

That was fair. However, I still hadn't determined where Roxy's true loyalties lay. "Last night, were you following me or Max?"

"Both. I wanted to find out what trouble Max was in, but I figured someone might have to save your butt when you got lost. I couldn't help but worry when you began talking to yourself."

A snort escaped me. "I was talking to my cat and a ghost," I explained like it was completely normal.

"Okaaay…" Her pierced eyebrow rose before she visibly juddered.

As though it were contagious, I shivered, caught in a wave of chills. While I suspected hers was an attack of the heebie-jeebies, mine was thanks to the crisp morning. After being out in the woods all night, my body struggled to keep itself warm even after the hot tea.

I shoved my hands into my pockets and felt cold metal graze my fingers. The ring Anita had given me to hold on to— I'd nearly forgotten about it. I played with it distractedly, sliding it on and off my thumb.

As we neared the end of the docks, I still wasn't ready to let Roxy off the hook, and my chance to get info out of her was slipping away. I remembered what she'd said the first night. *I want to find a pack to run with.* The wording must have been another private joke.

"So, do you want to be a part of Truce?"

She pulled a face. "Nah. They're too intense for me. But Max is my kind of people. Ever since I arrived on the island, he's had my back, so I look out for him in return. That is, when I'm not getting caught by Garrett's people and dragged in for questioning myself."

I forced a laugh, but her response reminded me that her connection with Max went beyond friendship to their shared ability to shift into animals. It was a part of him I'd never fully understand, not the way she and Teagan could. The knowledge seemed to wrench me further away from him, and a deep sense of loneliness crashed over me.

Roxy eyed me warily. "Do you want to interrogate me about the murder too?"

"No. I don't believe you did it." Although I'd said it before thinking, once it was out of my mouth, I knew it was true.

Her posture relaxed. "Good. Because I want to help. I'm not the detective you are, but I've got the morning off work. I can keep a bird's-eye view on the resort." She winked.

I laughed in earnest this time, but it morphed into a choke as a howl pierced the quiet. It was close. Too close.

Scanning our surroundings, I spotted a wolf waiting for us in the shadows, where the dock transitioned to land. Was it one of Garrett's people? Or Garrett himself? It was too far away to tell.

Roxy stared at me. "What's wrong?"

I took my hand out of my pocket and pointed ahead of us. "A wolf. Right there."

She followed my gaze and squinted. "There's nothing there."

If she couldn't see him, that meant it had to be my phantom friend. But that didn't make sense. "Didn't you just hear…"

I trailed off as the wolf opened its jaws again, this time without a sound. Hesitantly, I placed my hand back inside my pocket to touch the ring. I caught the tail end of its insistent baying before it swung around and ran off in the direction Max had gone.

My earlier theories about the creature formed into a solid conclusion. He was, in fact, a shifter. But not Levi as I'd first assumed.

This whole time, I'd believed the spirit was drawn by my ability to see him and possibly help him move on. However, it wasn't me he was interested in. It was Max. And the reason I could hear the animal by touching his father's ring pointed to only one explanation.

The wolf was Myles Nicolas.

So then where was Levi? Had he already moved on, or was

I looking for the wrong animal? I sucked in a sharp breath as the idea took hold.

"Are you okay?" Roxy asked me.

Slowly, I turned to her. "Yeah. I think I just realized something. The answer has been right in front of me this whole time. Levi wasn't a wolf like his sister, was he?"

"No." She gave me a strange look, losing that cool edge a little. Then she confirmed the suspicion that was taking root in my mind. "He was a lynx."

CHAPTER TWENTY

My shoes skidded on the rocky beach as I halted in front of the sheriff's caution tape. I positioned myself out of the security camera's view and surveyed the scene. The deck's jumbled remains stared back at me, unchanged. And yet, with my new knowledge, everything had changed.

I checked for witnesses. No one was in sight, not even Jason. He was probably grabbing a nap after guarding the deck all night, assuming no one would mess with the crime scene in broad daylight. Obviously, he'd underestimated my persistence.

"Levi, are you there?" I asked as loudly as I dared.

He had to be. He just had to. It was the only place I'd seen him. It made me wonder if it was because he was responsible for its collapse. Or perhaps this was the actual site of his death. Either way, one thing was now certain: the two events were connected.

I scanned the debris, searching for a glimpse of Levi's stubby tail or fur-tipped ears, but it was no use. The sun was rising higher by the moment and would make ghost hunting nearly impossible. As if being unable to hear him wasn't enough of a complication.

Desperate, I made a clicking sound with my tongue. "Here, kitty, kitty, kitty."

That was the most insulting thing I've ever heard, Zelda said.

I turned to find her slinking up behind me. "I wasn't talking to you. Apparently, Levi was a lynx shifter, so the ghost hanging around here has to be him."

She sat next to me, tucking her tail close to her body. *Huh. I guess, since a shifter's animal form is as much a part of them as their human form, that makes sense.*

"Oh, does that make sense?" I asked sarcastically. "Would have been nice if I'd known about the shifters earlier. I could have made the connection myself."

Her ears flattened pathetically against her head. *You know, I didn't go to Truce with you because I was sure you'd be safe with Max. Plus, they were more likely to spare you since it's harder to hide a human death.*

"Gee, that's comforting."

I mean that your death would be a murder. But when they look at me, they only see their next meal.

I blinked. The familiar usually acted so tough. It must have been difficult to admit she'd been afraid. "You're not exactly a sitting duck. You have powers."

It's not like I can shoot laser beams from my tail. My magic has limits. They're predators, and I'm just a cat.

It wouldn't win awards as far as apologies went, but I knew it was all I'd get from her. To her credit, she appeared sheepish.

I lowered myself to her level and sat on the stony beach. My clothes were already dirty from my midnight hike anyway. "You're not *just* a cat. And besides, I like to think if I'd truly been in trouble, you would have helped."

Her ears perked. *Yeah… Yeah, sure. So you're not mad?*

"Not about that."

She averted her golden gaze. *Okay, and I suppose I could have told you about the shifters in advance. But keeping Max's secret was important to Nolan.* Her furry chin rose with a hint of stubbornness.

I took a deep breath and tried to word my response carefully. While their bond would have broken upon his death, the fact he was still here made moving on complicated for her. If anyone understood that, it was me. "I know you're Nolan's familiar and not mine, but if we're going to work together, I need to trust you, and last night, you threw me to the wolves."

Yes, I see that now. I promise I won't put you in harm's way again. Not knowingly, anyway, she said, seeming sincere. At least until she added, *I wouldn't want to lose my source of tuna.*

I rolled my eyes. "Where's Nolan? I should clear the air with him too."

He went back to town.

My heart sank a little, but I wondered if it was for the best that he'd gone. His recent behavior had been odd—like his reluctance to help Max or the way he'd made me feel like I was nothing more than his ticket to the afterlife. His presence was beginning to make me feel uncomfortable. You know, more than ghosts usually did.

"Am I imagining things? Or is Nolan different as a ghost? A little more selfish, immature. I mean, I would get why," I added. "But is his recent behavior new, or am I seeing a different side to him?"

Probably a little of both. She tilted her head thoughtfully. *Nolan was my person, and I care very much for him, but he wasn't perfect. You're also not the twenty-two-year-old blushing bride anymore, so you might see things more clearly now.*

Her words stirred my earlier guilt. I picked up a rock and tossed it into the gentle waves licking the shore. "Yeah. I know it's not fair that I've been able to grow up and he hasn't."

Whoa. Don't get all sappy on me, she said. *I wasn't saying it's anything to feel guilty about. Life goes on. You've been doing the best you can, given everything that happened.*

I laughed humorlessly. "If running away for five years was the best I could do, I'd hate to see the worst."

She hopped onto my thigh and raised a paw as if to comfort me. Then she whacked me across the face.

Wake up, witch. I'm not talking about the best you're capable of—which would still be less than me on my worst day, I might add.

I rubbed my cheek. "Is this supposed to be a pep talk?"

After Nolan died, you did the best you could in that moment. Now, you're doing the best you can in this moment, which, after years of healing, is better than before. But you can't do better than your best. Which, again, is not as good as me.

Despite my stinging cheek, I took her words to heart. Perhaps it was because the sage advice came from Nolan's own familiar. Or else it was the fact she rarely offered a kind word.

I thought back to when I'd left the island. I'd lost my fiancé. Max, the man I normally would have leaned on, had confessed his love for me, and I'd felt like the worst person in the world for loving him back. It had broken me, so I'd gone away to heal. I wouldn't blame someone else for doing the same thing. So why was I blaming myself?

Zelda raised her paw again. I flinched, wary of another slap, but she turned my head to face the deck. That was when I spotted the lynx stalking back and forth among the wreckage.

I looked up. Heavy clouds had rolled in while we'd talked, threatening rain. Thanks to the cover, Levi appeared almost solid. However, that made it more unnerving when he swung his sharp focus toward us. His ears twitched with irritation, like Zelda's when I didn't open her tuna can fast enough.

Still avoiding the camera, I inched closer to the animal on my hands and knees, hoping he had the same level of awareness as Myles. "Levi. I'm Max's friend, Violet. I'm here to help you."

The big cat stilled in front of me. Now that I held his attention, I needed to figure out the best way to communicate. But when the right approach didn't come to mind, I settled for any way possible.

"Put up your paw if you know who killed you."

Zelda threw her head back and cackled. *Are you seriously trying to play charades with him?*

I glared at her. Levi dismissed me to resume his agitated pacing as though he were a caged animal, trapped not by walls but by his emotional ties to the scene. Okay, so he wasn't a big charades fan.

I tried again. "We're trying to solve your murder. Your family wants answers, and both Max and your sister are suspects. I know you don't want to see either of them in jail." *Unless Teagan actually killed you*, I amended in my mind.

He blinked at me once. Twice. Then he bounded off.

Curious, I followed him to the back of the building. He loped across the parking lot, straight for Max's truck. When I caught up to him, he paced at the rear of the vehicle, flicking his tail impatiently.

"I don't understand," I told him. "Max had nothing to do with your death."

In response, Levi swiped at the truck's bumper. His furry paw passed right through, but his message was clear. He wanted me to open it.

Apparently, I wasn't too off base with my charades idea. I gave Zelda an "I told you so" look before nearing the truck.

The contents of the bed hid beneath a hard-shell topper. Between the dark tint of the windows and mud splatter from the forestry roads, it was impossible to peer inside. I tried the tailgate's handle, expecting it to be locked. I was surprised when it popped open.

Biting my bottom lip, I lowered the gate. I wasn't sure what Levi had imagined I'd find, but there were only tools and an assortment of odds and ends: lumber, paint-splattered tarps, an axe.

Out of the corner of my eye, I caught a flash of red

darting through the sky toward me. A cardinal landed on the back of the truck. It appeared Roxy had started her surveillance.

Zelda suddenly sprang onto the tailgate. Ears tucked against her head, she slunk closer to the red bird with the same hungry look she usually wore at dinnertime.

I held out my hand to block her. "If you ever want to be fed again in your life, this bird is off limits."

With a growl, she lay down, tucking her paws under her chest. *I wasn't going to kill it. Only play a little.*

When I was certain the cat was going to behave, I scanned the truck bed one last time. Seeing nothing, I tried to shoo Zelda away so I could close it, but that intensity was back in her eyes again. This time, though, she zeroed in on the truck's contents.

Leaning forward, she waved her nose back and forth. *I smell blood.*

"W-What?"

I followed her gaze to a rusty hammer. Or at least I thought it was rust until I looked closer. Blood splatter.

Roxy must have noted it too, because she hopped around, wings fluttering.

Guess we found the murder weapon, Zelda said.

"Max didn't kill Levi. So that means whoever did planted this hammer to set him up."

So what do we do now?

Blowing out a long breath, I weighed my options. The murder weapon might have the killer's DNA or fingerprints all over it. But if I handed it over, the sheriff would arrest Max on the spot, and the murderer had likely wiped it clean before planting it. What was I supposed to do?

Something scuffed the pavement nearby. Roxy released a sharp trill of alarm and took flight. Levi bolted into the woods, as if anyone but Zelda and me could see him.

Incoming, Zelda hissed as she zipped under the truck.

"Violet?" Jason inquired. "What are you——"

His words cut short as he drew up beside me and focused on what hid in the back of the truck. His chiseled features slackened then formed a scowl, proving his powers of observation were quicker than mine.

I crouched to peer under the truck and locked eyes with Zelda before mouthing the words, "Warn Max."

She streaked toward the lodge at the same time as Roxy shot across the parking lot like an arrow. Hopefully, between the two of them, they'd find Max and get him away from the resort long enough for me to find the real murderer.

Jason must have misinterpreted my reaction as shock because he helped me to my feet and led me to a nearby bench. "Vi, I'm so sorry. I tried to warn you about Max. I wish you didn't have to find out this way. Why don't you take it easy while I contact the sheriff?"

Nodding, I sat on the bench, hands balled into fists to keep from shaking. I counted down the seconds, waiting until he wandered back to the truck before disobeying the order. Then I beelined it for Trent's office—my only remaining lead.

CHAPTER TWENTY-ONE

I shoved Trent's office door open and stormed inside, my brain rounding the bases with thoughts of dirty money, corrupt investors, and coverups. However, that all screeched to a halt, and so did I, when I found Trent and Alice on his desk, rounding second base.

Gasping, I covered my eyes. "Oh, I… Sorry."

As they clambered down, surprised grunts and urgent whispers filled the office, punctuated by a pen holder spilling its contents onto the floor. When the sounds died down, I peeked to make sure the coast was clear.

Trent smoothed his tie as a blush crawled out from beneath his collar. "Well, this is awkward."

Alice looked a little pink herself. "Vi, I'm so happy you're back safe, but what are you doing in here?"

I gave her my most apologetic grimace. "I'm sorry to interrupt, but this can't wait. It's about the investigation."

She gave me a subtle shake of her head, begging me with those puppy-dog eyes. "Please. Don't."

"It can't wait any longer," I told her. "They're going to arrest Max."

Her expression flickered from one emotion to the next.

Finally, her shoulders sagged, and she nodded. Hugging herself, she approached the window and stared at the view as though she wanted no part in this. However, her tense posture made it clear she was listening intently.

She obviously really liked the guy. I just hoped those feelings weren't misplaced.

Trent's gaze shifted between the two of us. "What is this about?"

"It's about the bag of cash Mayor Abernathy gave you."

His cheeks drained of color. "You know about that?"

"Yes." I wasn't about to explain how I knew. "What was the money for?"

He crumpled into his chair, elbows on the desk and head in his hands. "It was for throwing away my values."

Alice's chin dipped as she hugged herself tighter. She'd clearly been holding out hope he was squeaky clean. But while I knew she was hurting, I had to press on for Max's sake.

"Did it have something to do with Levi's murder?"

"What?" He gaped at me. "No. Nothing as terrible as that. It was payment for his daughter's wedding. They want to hold it here at the resort. It's part of the reason he's been putting so much pressure on me to get the place up and running. It had nothing to do with Levi. I swear."

I placed my hands on his desk and leaned in. "Then why are you acting as guilty as if it were?"

"Because it's not the first time I've accepted cash from him." His attention flicked to Alice, who still stared out the window, before dropping to his lap. "In the beginning, I tried to make up excuses, tell myself it was his way of investing, but after a while, it felt like…"

"Bribes?" I suggested.

"Something like that. I knew I shouldn't have taken it. Now, he's got me by the throat. And I suspect it won't end after his daughter's wedding."

"Why did you take it in the first place?"

"Normally, I wouldn't have. I've always prided myself on how I do business, but with all the bad luck we've had, this project has been a money pit from the start. The investors are pressuring me. Meanwhile, I have a couple hundred employees counting on a paycheck, and many of the island's small businesses are relying on the success of Siren's Call."

Trent rose and opened the closet door. The duffel bag was still there, like he hadn't wanted to touch it since stashing the money. He plopped it onto the desk and opened it before waving a hand to give me permission to look. But I'd already seen inside.

He sneered at the stacks of paper. "When you have all the answers to your problems right in front of you, it's hard to say no. Especially when the mayor is breathing down your neck. He's been instrumental in making this place happen, acting as my liaison with the local council members and greasing wheels. He says I owe him, that he could make the resort, my career, disappear. And I believe it."

Finally, Alice came to stand by Trent. His face creased as though he were bracing himself for an emotional blow. Instead, she placed her palms on either side of his face.

"Don't be so hard on yourself. Everyone makes mistakes. What matters now is what you do to fix it. You can fix it, right?" Her hopeful eyes searched his.

Trent's body sagged with relief. "Absolutely. I'll pay everything back. Well, as long as the killer is found and the grand opening gets back on track. If it doesn't…"

The ending to that sentence was clear: he'd be ruined.

Alice fixed me with an imploring look, as if my vote were the deciding factor. I stared at the small fortune in the bag. Maybe it wasn't enough to save a disgraced resort, but it would save a family business like Charming Treasures. Anyone who said it didn't tempt them would be lying.

On my return to Hope, I'd discovered our family-owned shop was teetering on the brink of bankruptcy, and my dad, one of the most principled men I knew, had considered committing insurance fraud to save it. Did that make him a terrible person? No. So how could I stand in front of Alice as judge, jury, and executioner for Trent when I'd done everything in my power to hide my dad's misstep?

"You're not the only one on this island who's gotten mixed up with Abernathy," I told him. "How do you think he greased so many wheels for the resort? But if you really want to do what's best for the investors and the community, you need to give the money back. There are rumors he's been siphoning money from the local treasury. The last thing you need is to get caught up in that."

He bobbed his head. "I'll fix this. You have my word."

Alice smiled at him, and he straightened, reminding me of a wilted flower turning to the sun. I knew he'd follow through on his promise, if not to ease his inner torture then to never lose the sensation of that warmth on his face.

After a moment, he refocused on me. "I'm sorry I don't have more answers for you. I wish I could help Max. Really, I do."

I gnawed on my lip, wondering where to search for answers next. If Trent wasn't involved in the murder, then we needed to figure out who'd planted the weapon in Max's truck. That was when the obvious solution hit me.

"Maybe you still can. Will you show me the security footage again?"

"Absolutely." He sprang into action.

After stashing the duffel bag in the closet, he stuck his head out the lobby door and called over to the front desk. A second later, Penelope entered, hugging her tablet as usual.

She eyed Alice and me before turning to her boss. "What can I do for you?"

Trent gestured to me, indicating I should take things from there.

"I'd like to see security footage from the last couple of days," I told her. "Specifically of Max's truck."

"Of course." She plopped in front of the computer.

I rounded the desk and hovered over her shoulder as she opened the program. Within minutes, we were staring at the front of Max's truck.

"Is there another camera angle where we can see the back?" I asked.

"No, sorry."

I frowned. "It will have to do."

One by one, we viewed each clip. They mostly showed Max going back and forth to grab tools from his truck. He was careful to lock it each time, which made it even stranger I'd found it unlocked. The occasional employee cut through the lot on their way to the staff cabins, but no one paused near the vehicle. My hope waned until we came to a video recorded the night before.

When Penelope hit Play, everything appeared in shades of gray thanks to the night mode. I worried it would be difficult to make anything out until a white blur entered the shot, headed straight for the truck.

The form came into focus. A wolf, white as snow against the dull-gray tones. It had to be Teagan.

The time stamp said one-thirty a.m. Max and I had been in Truce. I recalled how Teagan had shown up near the end of the meeting in the yurt, out of breath. Had she doubled back to the resort after escorting Max to Garrett? If she'd hurried, she could have stolen his keys, planted the hammer, and returned to Truce like she'd been there all along. It would explain why we'd found the keys away from his clothes.

Penelope moved the curser to close the video. "Sorry. The motion detection can't tell the difference between human and animal."

"Wait," I told her. "Keep playing it."

Probably thinking I was a little too excited about the local wildlife activity, she did as I asked. I leaned closer. This had to be it.

In a perfect world, we'd witness the wolf transforming into a human to unlock the tailgate, and though I'd have some explaining to do, I could identify them. But it disappeared behind the truck, completely blocked from sight. A few seconds passed before the vehicle rocked on its struts. Eventually, the animal scurried away.

"Can you go back to the start and pause it?" I asked. "Just as the wolf comes into view?"

Penelope raised her eyebrows but didn't argue. She restarted the video then paused it as the creature's massive head turned to face the screen. While most would see a wolf nervous around human territory, I saw a shifter on the lookout for witnesses.

Alice peered closer. "What's in its mouth?"

"A stick?" Trent guessed. "Or a bone?"

But I already knew what it was. A hammer. And if we could have zoomed in with crystal clarity, we'd likely have seen a set of keys dangling from its jaws too.

A firm knock on the door made us all jump, and Jason's voice filtered into the office. "Mr. Bass? It's Deputy Swan."

Trent straightened to answer it. "Coming."

I laid a hand on his arm. "Wait. Let me sneak out the other door first. I'm certain I can smoke out the murderer in Truce, but Jason will try to stop me."

Alice gaped at me. "You can't go wandering through the forest again. It's not safe."

"She's right," Trent said. "These woods are dangerous. So I'll drive you."

I wasn't sure what I'd been expecting, but it hadn't been that. Stunned, I simply stared back. "Thank you."

Alice threw her arms around him and kissed his cheek.

Penelope leaped out of the chair. "You can't, Trent. You have a conference call with the investors in an hour, and with everything going on, you don't want to miss that. I'll drive her." She fished a set of keys out of the desk drawer and gave them a jingle.

I'd never heard a sweeter sound. "What are we waiting for?"

CHAPTER TWENTY-TWO

I bounced and jostled in the passenger seat as the SUV navigated the rough and muddy forestry roads to Truce. With each fork in the road, Penelope concentrated harder on our path, her electric-blue fingernails tapping anxiously against the steering wheel. The cab was silent but for the wipers swishing back and forth. The downpour had started when I was in Trent's office and was making the journey precarious—as if our destination wasn't dangerous enough.

While Teagan was guilty of planting the murder weapon in Max's truck, I wasn't convinced she'd killed her brother, though it was possible she knew who had. But why help frame someone else? Wouldn't she want justice for Levi? Unless the person who'd murdered him was the one person she'd vowed to protect: Garrett.

Anita had said the people of Truce weren't so much loyal to their leader as they were afraid of him. If they knew about him killing one of their own, would they turn against him? I sure hoped so, or I was handing myself over on a silver platter. It was a thought I didn't want to dwell on.

Eager to distract myself, I shifted my focus to Penelope.

"So, tell me more about yourself. You said you're from the island, right?"

"That's right," she said. "After moving away as a kid, I've always wanted to come back. I'm thankful Trent gave me the opportunity to."

"Did you go to school in Hope?"

She threw me a sideways look. "Are there any other options? You know, unless you want to live in Serenity."

We both wrinkled our noses at the mention of Hope's rival town then laughed. It seemed even after all those years away, she still had that local spirit.

As we crested the rise, she slowed the vehicle and drew in a breath. "It's beautiful. I haven't seen this view for almost twenty years, but it's exactly as I remember it."

We were perched at the top of the rocky ridge, and the inlet spread out below us, clear and expansive. Siren's Call was barely visible, camouflaged as it was. Trent had done a good job minimizing the resort's impact on the area.

After a moment, she reluctantly drove on, plunging us down the other side of the mountain and back into the forest. "We're close to Truce. We'll be there in a couple of minutes."

When I spotted smoke rising from chimneys ahead, I fidgeted in my seat. "You should pull over here. I'll walk in by myself."

"Are you sure?"

I wasn't, but it was risky enough for me to be there. I didn't want to drag another outsider into the mess any more than I already had. Especially a human. "I'm sure. Hopefully, I won't be long. Stay with the vehicle, and keep the engine running." Although I tried to sound casual, I felt anything but.

When the SUV came to a stop, I hopped out and pulled up my jacket hood, but it wasn't waterproof, and the downpour soaked me in ten seconds flat. With a wave to Penelope, I shut the vehicle door as quietly as I could. However, as I made my way to the center of the village, movement among the trees told me I'd never had a chance of sneaking in. Garrett probably had sentries placed around the village, and a bird shifter would have spied our vehicle from miles away. I hoped Penelope would be all right.

Keeping my focus ahead, I picked up the pace. I didn't want anyone stopping me before I tracked down my suspect.

Keep cool, Vi.

"What do you think you're doing here?" a voice hissed behind me.

A scream threatened to tear from my lungs, but when I wheeled around and found Nolan stalking toward me, I swallowed it back down. So much for keeping it cool. Maybe I'd aim for lukewarm.

Thanks to the trees dotting the village and the heavy clouds, my fiancé took on a solid appearance as if he were really there with me. While I wanted to be annoyed about it, nothing but gratitude filled me. At least someone was there to have my back—in spirit, anyway.

"I'm doing what I always planned to do," I said. "Clear Max's name. And I'm not leaving, so you can either help me or risk losing your only hope of moving on."

He cringed and stared down at his expensive shoes. "Sorry I said it that way. I didn't mean for it to sound like it's the only reason I was worried about you."

I wasn't sure if he was sorry because that wasn't the only reason or because it was and he just didn't want me to know. This new side to Nolan was making me question everything I thought I knew about him. Either way, I didn't have time to deal with it.

I continued walking. "I thought you were returning to Hope."

Falling into step beside me, Nolan rubbed the back of his neck. "I was on my way there, but I decided you were right. I was being selfish. Max needs my help to clear his name. So I came here to see if I could learn anything."

"And did you?"

"Nothing specific, but Teagan has been acting cagey." He glanced back at my ride. "By the way, the woman who drove you here looks familiar. Have we met her before?"

"Not that I remember. She lived on the island when she was young, though, so you might recognize her from school."

"That's probably it. It bugs me when I can't put a name to a face."

I rolled my eyes. "I know you were Mr. Popular and all, but you didn't know everyone."

"True." He waggled an eyebrow at me. "But everyone wanted to know me."

I smirked, relieved to see a glimpse of the old Nolan. "I'm glad you're here." Then bittersweet nostalgia punched me in the guts to remind me he wasn't truly there.

"But you shouldn't be here. Truce is too dangerous. Please, Vi. It's not too late to go back."

"The killer has to be from Truce. I can't stand by and let Max take the fall. I've turned my back on him once already, and I won't do it again."

A curious expression crossed his face, but whatever he wanted to say, he kept to himself. "I hope you have a plan."

"Um, sort of. I'll work it out as I go." I strode on with more confidence than I felt.

As we closed in on the center of the village, more houses popped up around us. Both humans and animals peered out of windows and doors to scrutinize me. Despite the downpour, many filtered out of their homes to follow, Anita among them, her worry lines deepening as she watched me.

From the deep shade of the tree line, a wolf emerged. Max's dad. Instead of leading the charge, he fell into step beside me. I supposed that meant he was there to support me in whatever ghostly way he could. But since he was never far from his son, I wondered if he was really there for me or if Max was somewhere nearby.

Remembering the Nicolas family ring, I pulled it out of my pocket and slipped it onto my thumb. While it wasn't like I'd be able to understand Myles in wolf form, it made me feel less alone to be connected to him.

By the time my invisible entourage and I arrived at the yurt, Garrett was standing with Teagan and Shane beneath the awning's protection. Scratching his beard absently, he waited for the parade of people behind me to gather around. Or perhaps they were boxing me in.

He eyed me as if I were dinner. "I don't recall extending an open invitation during your last visit."

Ignoring the flutter of panic in my stomach, I stood straighter. "I'm here to expose Levi's murderer."

"You won't find them here." He surveyed his "loyal" subjects gathering around us. "We don't kill our own kind. We look out for one another here."

Ironic, since he'd killed Myles. "And you do that by planting evidence on one of your own?"

He didn't even flinch. A perfect poker face. "I don't know what you're talking about. But why don't we step inside, out of the rain?"

Teagan and Shane reached out to "help" me comply, but I stepped away.

"I don't think so." I raised my voice. "Everyone should hear this. Unless, of course, you have something to hide from your people. Or maybe Teagan acted all by herself when she hid the murder weapon in Max's truck."

Our audience buzzed with surprise, and hushed whispers trickled all the way to the back. Myles growled, low and menacing, as though demanding an explanation from Teagan.

Okay, so I was only ninety percent sure it had been her in the video, but my poker face must have been pretty good too, because she didn't deny it.

She cocked her blond head. "I won't apologize. The investigation wasn't going anywhere, and my brother deserved justice, so I helped it along."

"If you're so certain it was Max, why didn't you go straight to the sheriff?"

Garrett stepped forward. "Our kind sticks together. I wished to keep the matter in the pack and deal out our own punishment. I brought Max here and gave him the opportunity to confess, but he denied it. So I had Teagan sniff out where he'd tossed the hammer into the woods and asked her to return his property, ensuring the authorities found their man."

I crossed my arms. "Or the man you wanted them to. What proof do you have he's the murderer, other than the evidence you planted on him?"

"I saw him kill Levi in the marina with my own two eyes." He said it like his word was enough proof. "Now, this interview is finished. However, it's time we deal with your trespassing." He snapped his fingers at Teagan and Shane, who instantly converged on me.

Afraid they'd drag me away before the truth came out, I reached for my only weapon: their fear of my power. I faced Myles, who was close at my heel. "I don't think he's telling the truth. Do you?"

The wolf's snarled response hinted at a great big no.

I shrugged at Garrett. "Your old leader doesn't believe so either."

In the middle of grabbing for my arm, Shane snatched his hand away as if I were infectious, and Teagan took a step back. Unease rippled through the surrounding crowd, and people scanned the area as though they might see Myles in the flesh. Garrett tried to remain impassive, but I didn't miss how his focus darted around too.

"There's one problem with your eyewitness account," I said. "The resort's security footage shows you stayed in your room all afternoon until the party."

"So? That's where I witnessed the murder. From my room."

A-ha! I had him. "Your room is on the fourth floor, facing the mountains. There's no way you saw the marina from there. And if you're lying about that, what else are you lying about?" I pretended to think. "For example, if you didn't actually see Levi die, how did you know a hammer was the murder weapon?"

Teagan's hard expression slackened as she refocused on her leader. "You lied to me." She looked genuinely shocked.

Garrett spread his arms. "Teagan. Come on. We both know he's guilty."

I stepped closer to him, and no one moved to stop me. "It's natural you'd want to blame Max for it. You've hated him for years because his existence threatens your right to leadership and, let's face it, your pride."

"There is no threat!" he roared, causing those nearby to shrink back. "I am the leader!"

Nolan shifted uncomfortably. "That's enough, Vi. It doesn't matter if everyone here knows the truth if you get ripped to shreds."

"I've got this," I muttered.

Fury rolled off Garrett, and my insides shriveled. I knew I should stop, but he was so close to cracking. *One more push.*

"You were only in charge because Max allowed it. Being the leader by default wasn't enough. Sending him to jail would get him out of the way permanently. Plus, the murder was an awfully convenient way to take care of your other threat—the resort. Were you behind the deck collapsing too?"

The murmurs and whispers gave way to shouts as his people demanded answers. It bolstered my nerve. They wanted the truth. They deserved to understand who was leading them.

"I don't need to answer to you!" Then Garrett wheeled to face those who dared speak against him. "I don't need to answer to anyone here."

"Maybe not," I said. "You will have to answer to the sheriff, though. And they know I'm here, so if I don't return, they'll come looking for me."

"The sheriff has no power here." He stalked toward me.

I backed away but came to a halt as I bumped into the edge of the crowd. No one moved to let me through, and my stomach dropped. Had I underestimated the alpha's power over them?

Nolan threw himself in front of me and tried shoving Garrett in the chest, but his ghostly arms just slipped through his thick torso. Garrett shuddered at the sensation. It only made him seem excited at the prospect of killing me.

My earlier confidence evaporated. *I don't have this. I so don't have this!*

Garrett's hand shot out, his fingernails nicking my skin as he grasped me by the arm. No. Not fingernails. Claws. He was already mid-shift.

He pulled me close enough that the force of his words hurled a mix of rain and spittle into my face. "There's only one person Truce pack members answer to, and that's me." He bared a pair of incisors that lengthened before my eyes.

Fear locked my limbs in place.

"No. They answer to their leader," a voice called out. A blissfully familiar voice. Max.

Garrett's hold on me eased, and he searched for the source of the voice. Heads craned as everyone else did the same until, finally, the crowd parted and Max emerged.

A hush fell over the throng as he strolled up, jaw clenched with determination, steely gaze unwavering. "So I challenge you for leadership. And when I win, you'll answer to me for your crimes."

Garrett shoved me aside and squared off with Max until they were nose to nose. "You want to be leader? You're not one of us anymore, traitor. Who will stand behind you?"

His smug expression sagged as, one by one, more and more

of his people stepped forward. Anita appeared next to her son, glowing with pride.

Garrett's face twisted, and a growl tore from his lips. "So be it." He spun on his heel and stalked into the yurt, calling back over his shoulder. "It's your funeral."

CHAPTER TWENTY-THREE

Swept along with the rest of the villagers, Max, Anita, Nolan, and I entered the yurt. Garrett was draped casually across his carved throne, the front of his fur cloak splayed open to expose his bare chest. Based on the bored look on his face, you'd think the villagers had gathered for a meeting about garbage collection schedules, not to watch two alphas tear each other apart.

Wham!

The giant wooden doors slammed, shutting out the rest of the world. My heart careened around my chest, and my vision struggled to adjust to the flickering torchlight.

So many bodies—human and furry—crowded the stands. The chatter and scents accosted me, while the anger and confusion from their collective souls grated against my powers in a way I'd never experienced.

Max gave his mother a hug before turning to me. "Are you going to be all right?"

Was *I* going to be all right? He should have been worried about himself. I gripped him by the collar. "Please don't do this."

He gently removed my death grip. "Garrett won't let us walk out of Truce now. You shouldn't have come here."

"I-I thought I could get a confession out of him and prove your innocence before the sheriff arrested you. I'd hoped enough of the pack would be against him."

He pinched the bridge of his nose. "It's going to take more than accusations. No matter how much they hate him, they won't turn on him that easily. Remember, it's not about loyalty. It's instinct. The only way we're both getting out of this alive is if I win the fight."

My cheeks burned, and my eyes stung as I held back tears. "If you get hurt, I'll never forgive myself."

"This isn't your fault. This fight has been a long time coming. It's about much more than you or Levi or even my dad. It's about them." He gestured to those in the stands. "You were right. I despised the way they fell at Garrett's feet after he murdered my father, but they were following their natural impulses. I was just too stubborn to admit it. Garrett is a terrible leader, and I was wrong to abandon the village. My father would have wanted better for them. I want better for them. So it's time someone ends his reign, and I'm the only one who can do that."

"And if you can't?"

"We're both goners."

I swallowed hard. "Then I guess you'll have to win."

"I plan on it." With a wink, he turned and left, taking a piece of me with him.

Would those be the last words we'd ever speak to each other? There were more important things I wanted to express, but with Nolan present, they had to remain locked away. As it was, my fiancé stood back, watching me closely with the same curious expression he'd worn earlier, so I fought to keep my emotions from playing across my face.

Myles trailed behind Max until they passed the dais. He slowed to watch his son walk away, and his tail dipped briefly before he climbed the steps to take his rightful place.

Nolan came to stand next to me. "Don't worry. We've seen

Max get into enough scrapes over the years. He's tough. He can handle this."

I wanted to remind him he was referring to our high school days, that this wasn't a battle of egos in the empty lot next to Electri-fried Wings. This was life or death.

Tugging on my arm, Anita led me to the stands, where other villagers made space for her in the front row, behind a low partition. Nolan stood nearby for the best views, since he wasn't exactly blocking anyone's line of sight.

I sank next to Anita and squeezed her hand, partly to show my support and partly because I needed some myself. Despite the brave smile she plastered on, her features creased with worry. This poor woman had already lost her husband, and now, she faced the possibility of losing her son to the same man. And what if that was only the beginning? So far, Garrett had allowed her to live peacefully in the village. Would his hospitality end after this?

Natural light filtered in through circular openings in the ceiling that allowed the various animal scents and torch smoke to escape. I noted the lights placed at intervals overhead, enough to illuminate the place like a hockey arena.

"Does it have to be so dark?" I asked Anita. "Why all the moody torches when they can turn on the lights?"

"I believe it's for ambience, dear."

"Oh." Of course. Because you had to set the right mood when fighting to the death.

As we waited, Teagan approached us. She paused in front of Anita and dipped her head in a show of respect. Instead of moving on, she rounded the partition and sat stiffly next to me. I wondered if this was her way of publicly choosing sides. Several awkward seconds passed before I felt her study me out of the corner of her eye.

"Nervous?" she asked.

"Aren't you?"

"I'm resigned. This is what you came here for, isn't it? You wanted information."

I shook my head. "Not like this. Not at the risk of Max getting hurt."

"This is our way. If Max wins, we both get our answers. If Garrett wins, you and I will probably die. Either way, we'll have a resolution."

Her certainty sent shivers down my spine.

The crowd stirred, and I spotted Max's furry black form enter the open space. A gate closed behind him, locking into place with a heavy click of finality.

The collective energy rose, dragging my nerves along with it. People cheered or booed as those in animal form joined in with their own versions. By the mixed reactions, it was difficult to tell how many people supported or opposed Max.

Garrett stood to address those gathered. "You all know the rules. We fight until one of us yields or until there's no fight left in them." The corner of his mouth twitched into a cold sneer.

It brought to mind how Garrett had killed Max's father instead of simply defeating him, and I wondered... No. I was certain that was what he had in store for Max.

Now that Garrett was standing, Myles hopped onto the throne —the seat that had once been his. In fact, now that I knew who he really was, his behavior on my previous visit made sense. He hadn't relieved himself on Garrett because he didn't like him—okay, that might have been part of it. Myles had been marking his territory.

While canine facial expressions weren't exactly telling, I imagined the angst he hid beneath his wolfy mask matched his wife's, but he raised his snout in the air with a great show of composure and dignity.

As Garrett descended the stairs, he slid out of one fur coat at the same time as he changed into his other. When he hit the last step in full animal form, he bounded to the center to square off with Max.

They tensed, bodies taut, muscles quivering with coiled energy. The roar from the audience crescendoed. My seat vibrated with the stomping of feet until I couldn't tell if my trembling was from the jostling or my fear.

Breathless, I waited for the fight to start. I expected a gunshot or a series of drumbeats to count down. Instead, the arena hushed until only feral snarling from the opponents filled the space. Then, after the most painful minute of my life, the two wolves burst into action.

Garrett released like a spring, fangs bared. Max lunged a split second later. They collided in a whirlwind of fur and tumbled to the ground.

Wrestling in the dirt, each writhing mass tried to get the upper hand. Jaws snapped. Fierce growls tore from their lungs.

The russet wolf threw his weight around. He knocked Max to the floor, teeth encircling his neck. Anita's hand tightened around mine—or maybe it was the other way around. I held my breath, waiting for my worst fears to come true.

Garrett's jaws clamped down. Max yipped and twisted out of the lethal hold. His black fur glistened in the torchlight. Blood. Thankfully, the injury didn't seem to slow him down as he dove back into the fight.

Over and over, Garrett charged with bold and powerful moves. But while he might have been the larger of the two, Max was lithe and clever. His muscles sprang with raw energy, and he danced around his brutish opponent as though they were playing a game and he could do it all day.

Eventually, Garrett grew sluggish, shifting from an offensive rhythm to a defensive one. Hope surged through my veins until Nolan pointed across the arena. A gray blur raced across the dirt floor. It was Shane in his wolf form, cutting a straight path for the fight.

Heart stuttering, I jumped to my feet. "Max! Look out!"

My cry was swallowed by the crowd's uproar. People yelled foul and demanded a halt to the match, but no one seemed brave enough to intervene. Shane didn't falter, beelining it for the fight. Anita rose unsteadily while clutching me for support, and we watched, helpless.

Shane collided with Max, and they rolled in the dirt. Before my friend could scramble to his paws, the new wolf pounced and pinned him to the ground.

Max twisted this way and that, narrowly avoiding Shane's snapping teeth. However, he had no chance of beating someone so fresh in the fight. Meanwhile, Garrett lurched to all fours to catch his breath.

I turned to Teagan. "How is this allowed? Isn't it against the rules?"

But she was already vaulting over the partition, yanking her shirt over her head. She tossed it back, and it hit me in the face. By the time I'd pulled it away, she was in wolf form.

As she sprinted to join the fray, her bony wolf legs slipped out of her jeans. While she apparently went commando beneath her pants, the same could not be said for her upper half. To save time, she'd left on her sports bra. It resulted in a strange sight—a whole new level of wardrobe malfunction. Or maybe, in this case, animal cruelty.

Teagan shot across the arena like white-hot lightning and launched her furry body at Shane. The hit knocked him off Max, and he skidded across the dirt floor.

She leaped on top of him and forced him to the ground so he wasn't able to interfere again. But the damage had been done. Max's chest heaved with labored breaths. His shoulder appeared wetter than before, and each step left a dark stain on the ground.

Would he have enough energy to finish the fight?

Max faced off against Garrett once more. They circled each other, growling something only they could decipher. With a confident curl to his wolfy muzzle, the russet wolf lunged. My insides twisted.

Barely moving, Max stepped aside like a butterfly dodging

a locomotive. Then, using Garrett's momentum against him, he pounced from behind. In a flash, the leader was down, Max's deadly jaws around his neck.

Garrett clawed at Max, trying to regain control. Once, twice. He failed. There was no room for escape.

It was over.

Anita cried out in relief, and I whooped in triumph. However, my joy faded when the fight didn't end.

Max's sharp teeth sank farther into Garrett's neck. The leader yelped. Blood stained his russet fur. As he writhed and wriggled to free himself, the toothy trap tightened, and he let out a pathetic whimper.

The audience screamed, some for blood and some for mercy. Anita's grip on my hand tightened. I waited for Max to back down, but he didn't.

When he'd challenged Garrett the first time, he'd wanted revenge for his father's death. In the years since, he'd been exiled from the pack, branded as a traitor, and now, framed for murder. This time, would he finish the job?

A nauseating few seconds passed. Gnawing on my lip, I twisted my hair around my finger so hard it hurt. Finally, Max released his fatal hold and backed away to lick his chops.

The yurt erupted in a mixture of noises. Most sounded like cheers. Whether it was for Max's win or the exhilaration of the spectacle, I couldn't tell.

Nolan tried to tap my arm excitedly, though I felt so numb I hardly registered the temperature change. "See? I told you he'd win. Good old Max."

Had he been watching a different fight? Garrett had nearly killed Max. Had he lost all sense of how precious life was?

Anita let go of my hand, which tingled from a lack of circulation. We embraced, and her tears soaked through the shoulder of my shirt. While people gathered around her son to congratulate him, she seemed unable to move, so I remained by her side.

My attention drifted to the wooden throne. Myles had remained there the entire time, never trying to interfere. Maybe because he understood the rules or because he'd been confident his son would come out the victor.

Tongue lolling, his mouth formed a wolfy smile. He tilted his head back and released a howl only I could hear thanks to the signet ring. The sound pierced the air, rising above the rest of the clamor.

His form glowed with an ethereal light. It intensified until it dispersed, leaving the echo of his triumphant howl behind. Eventually, that faded too. Despite the cacophony, it left an impression of silence. Peace.

But there was no peace for the living, because the doors to the outside world suddenly burst open, and a guard called out, "The sheriff is approaching the village!"

CHAPTER TWENTY-FOUR

The celebration was cut short as people scattered. Or, more specifically, the animals did—wouldn't that have been a sight for the sheriff? I wasn't sure how much time we had before he arrived and arrested Max, but it would be the shortest leadership term in history. Determined not to let that happen, I marched over to Garrett.

By the time I approached the former leader, Max had transformed and stood partially clothed over his fallen rival. When he turned to face me, I flinched at the sight of him. A bruise blossomed across his cheek, and his right eye had swollen shut. Blood covered his left shoulder and raced down the contours of his bare chest to soak the waistband of his jeans.

I gaped at him. "Max, you need a doctor."

"I'll be fine." He chuckled. "Shifters heal fast, and we have more important things to attend to."

It was true. There was no time to waste. Not even on a bandage. I averted my gaze from his injuries and focused on the task ahead.

Garrett was still on the ground, recovering from the fight. Thankfully, someone had covered him with his fur cloak. He reached into its pocket and drew out his signet ring before sliding it onto his finger. Slowly, he pushed himself up to one knee, but judging by the sneer on his face, I doubted it was a sign of respect for his new leader. He simply looked too weak to rise any farther.

Nolan came to stand next to me. "Let Max do this. If you take over the interrogation, you'll undermine his new authority."

An argument surged to my lips, but I clamped them tight. He was right. Besides, what would I get out of Garrett that Max couldn't, especially after he'd just kicked his tail?

My friend stared down his nose at the disgraced leader. "Garrett Swift, did you kill Levi Ashwind? I command you to tell me."

The man flashed a self-assured grin. "I did not."

Max's face twitched with annoyance, but he tried again. "Did you sabotage the resort's deck?"

His smug look never wavered. "I did not."

"Did you order someone else to do it?"

"I did not." He sighed as if we were keeping him from his afternoon nap. "And I don't need to answer any more questions."

Max's nostrils flared. "You will if I command it."

"You're not my leader." He found the energy to rise, only faltering a little as he put weight on his right leg. "I renounce my ties to this pack."

Scandalized gasps ricocheted around me. Perhaps this was a coward's way out. Hadn't he called Max a traitor for leaving the pack, and now, he was doing the same? He was a hypocrite.

Max inhaled deeply through his nose. "Fine. If you won't answer to me, you'll be answering to the sheriff soon enough."

Garrett raised his chin. "I have nothing to say. I had no involvement in either crime."

"Something tells me you know who did."

"What evidence do you have?"

He had us there. There was no proof, and the sheriff was coming to arrest Max. Pack business or not, I wouldn't stand by and do nothing.

I stepped forward. "We don't have time for this. Let me see his ring."

Max quirked an eyebrow but didn't question me before approaching Garrett and holding out his hand. After some hesitation, the man reluctantly passed it over. The second Max laid it in my palm, Garrett's will hit me like a battering ram. If Teagan had been a brick wall keeping me out, he was an iron fortress.

I sensed everyone watching with fear, judgment… even disgust. Tuning them out, I closed my eyes and went to battle with Garrett's spirit. I clenched the ring as though I could physically punch my way through his barrier.

"Anything?" Nolan's voice broke through my concentration.

Unclenching my fist, I shook my head and lowered my voice. "I'm not powerful enough. His will is too strong."

My conversation with thin air sent whispers circling around me. Max silenced them with a wave of his hand.

Nolan held my gaze steadily. "You are powerful enough. You just haven't had enough practice yet. Try again. This time, don't go head-to-head with his spirit. Search for another way in, a back door, a soft spot."

Closing my eyes again, I kept my fist relaxed and my breathing even as I bumped against the spiritual wall. I moved purposefully, using my will to grope until I found a crack in his defenses. I wiggled through. A little farther. A peek was all I managed.

Garrett shaking a hand. A deal struck. Promises of forgiveness. That was all I got. Impressions and vague intentions. As soon as I returned to Hope, I was going to ask Helen to put me in the accelerated witch course.

The doors burst open again, yanking me out of my concentration. This time, Penelope stumbled in.

"The sheriff's here!" she panted.

As the room turned as one to check out the intruder, she recoiled at the scrutiny. What had she not understood about "Stay with the vehicle?" How on earth would I explain this scene to her?

She hugged herself as if wishing she had her tablet to hide behind. "What's going on?"

No one in the yurt seemed to know what to say. They simply stared at the outsider like a predator waiting for its prey to bolt and begin the chase. But she wasn't looking at any of them. Her focus was on Garrett.

Sure, he was standing before a group of angry spectators, bruised and bloody, but something told me her interest was more than curiosity. It was expectant, like she was waiting for him to answer her.

Reaching out to the ring again, I zeroed in on the hand Garrett shook. A woman's—with electric blue fingernails. My attention flew to Penelope's manicured hands. She wasn't here to warn me about the sheriff. She'd come to warn Garrett.

I recalled how she'd known the way to the village. Then there was what she'd said about the view before we arrived, that she hadn't seen it for almost twenty years. There was only one way the pack would have let her get so close to Truce.

Nolan snapped his fingers—which was physically impossible, not to mention disconcerting. "That's it! I remember her. She was a couple of grades below us. Quiet, always clutching her schoolbooks to her chest." He crossed his arms, miming it. "Kids used to call her something really mean because of her pronounced front teeth. Something like Bucky... Bucky Becky!"

"Becky?" I inquired, refusing to use the hurtful nickname.

Penelope's hands automatically flew up to cover her mouth.

"I-I don't go by Becky anymore. I changed my name after I got my teeth fixed."

But she'd lied, hidden her identity. Why? It felt like Nolan had thrown out a fishing line, so I reeled it in. "You're not just from the island, are you? You were part of the pack."

Max took a step forward, peering at her in the light filtering through the open doors as though seeing her for the first time. "Becky Rivers? I can't believe I didn't recognize you."

The onlookers murmured and whispered among themselves, perhaps finally placing her.

She shifted from foot to foot. "It's been a few years. My teeth weren't the only thing people made fun of me for, so I had a few other issues fixed." She briefly touched her nose.

We were minutes away from Max being arrested, and it felt like an awkward homecoming for this woman. I half expected someone to produce an elementary school yearbook. However, she didn't seem to grasp where this was going, so I kept reeling in the line, hoping I'd caught my big fish.

"I get it," I told her. "Kids tortured you in school, which must have been awful for you. You wanted a fresh start, a new look and name. But you never forgot about the place you called home." I spread my arms to indicate the surrounding village. "So when you found a ticket back to the island, you wanted a do-over."

Penelope hugged herself tighter. "Both my parents died a couple of years back. I felt so alone and remembered the good times I had here when I was a kid."

"You weren't welcomed back, though, were you?"

She ducked her head. "When I first ran into Garrett at one of his protest rallies, he said I'd disgraced the pack. That the resort was my fault since I'd suggested Charm Island to Trent. He told me I'd never be a part of the pack again unless I…"

"Fixed the problem you created?" I supplied.

Her eyes widened as she realized her mistake in opening up. I didn't give her a chance to backpedal out of it.

"As Trent's assistant, you could sabotage the project from the inside. That's how shipments disappeared and equipment malfunctioned. Then, when Siren's Call was complete, you took things to the next level. You sabotaged the deck to ruin the resort's reputation for good." The nickname suddenly made sense. Bucky, as in buck teeth. "You're a beaver shifter, aren't you?"

Max wrinkled his forehead, perhaps recalling my query about beavers the previous night. "They moved away so long ago I never made the connection."

She backed up to the open doors. Before she could slip out, Teagan blocked the exit with her body, glaring at Penelope as though daring her to try something. Her fists clenched and unclenched, but she held her position, waiting for the confession she'd been seeking.

Penelope's shoulders drooped. "When I swam up to the deck in beaver form, I knew that even if I chewed the support posts, there was no guarantee it would collapse. Then, I discovered Levi had left his tools behind. They were just lying there, the answer to my problems. I-I hoped gnawing the pillars would make it look like an accident, the result of messing with nature and nature fighting back."

"But Levi returned for his tools and caught you," I guessed.

"I didn't want to hurt him." Her body convulsed with a sob. "Even though I begged him not to tell, he was going to rat me out, so I grabbed his hammer and…" She sniffled. "After that, I shifted into a beaver and swam him far away. Or at least I assumed it was far enough. I didn't think… I didn't think anyone would ever find him." Succumbing to her tears, she collapsed to the floor.

A range of emotions flitted through the crowd. Their disgust and sense of betrayal as a community was so strong my powers sensed it. It was like a physical weight pressing me down, zapping my energy. But time was ticking away, so I pushed on.

"You drove Levi's truck back to the parking lot, knowing exactly how to avoid the security cameras. Did you hope people would assume Levi wandered off?"

At first, Penelope was crying too hard to answer. A few hiccups later, she found her voice. "I hoped they would blame it on a wolf attack. After all, you'd told the front desk you spotted one nearby." She studied the dirt floor. "No body. No evidence leading to Truce or anyone in particular."

"Except Teagan," I said. "She went down to the deck to talk to Levi. You deleted that clip before reviewing the footage with the sheriff, didn't you? But you missed the video of Max walking straight for Levi's truck after he disappeared, so he looked like the last person to see him alive."

"I never meant for Max to appear guilty." She turned her red-rimmed eyes to him. "I'm so sorry."

His lips pursed. "Maybe you didn't, but Garrett saw an opportunity to take down his rival and acted on it. And something tells me he was pulling the strings all along." He faced Garrett. "You knew Penelope was desperate to rejoin the pack, so you used her to sabotage the resort."

The man lifted a shoulder. "If she interpreted things that way, it was her mistake. And as the witch pointed out, there's footage proving I was in my room the whole time. In fact, until that afternoon, I'd never stepped foot on the property, so you can't tie me to any sabotage."

Penelope's mouth popped open. "You told me that if I helped you—"

"That what?" He sneered. "You could rejoin a pack of magical animals? Is that what you'll tell the sheriff?" He shook his head at all of us. "I won't even go down for conspiring to set up Max, since a wolf planted the evidence. You've got nothing on me."

Nolan huffed. "He's right. He won't see any jail time."

Max crossed his arms. "But we know the truth. And in

Truce, we take care of our own." The growl in his voice raised the hairs on my arms.

Garrett tensed as though he might try to fight again. "You'll have to catch me first."

In a move faster than I'd expected after his beating, he shifted into his wolf form. His paws hit the ground, and he sprinted for the exit.

Hands stretched out to grab him, but he slipped past them all. Teagan braced herself in front of the doors like a goalie protecting a soccer net. As he neared, she leaped on top of him.

He kicked and clawed himself free before dashing outside. Teagan cursed and got to her feet, wiping a streak of blood off her cheek where Garrett had scratched her.

Max ordered a handful of villagers to follow him as if commanding them was the most natural thing in the world. Although his ability to take charge didn't surprise me, the confidence and ease with which he did it sucked the air from my lungs.

As for the villagers, they obeyed without question, disappearing into the woods. I assumed they'd shift once they were far enough away. However, something told me they wouldn't find Garrett.

A stillness settled over the group, interrupted by gravel crunching beneath tires. The low timbre of the sheriff's muffled words floated on the air as he spoke with someone outside. We'd run out of time.

Teagan shut the doors, plunging us into near darkness again. She dropped a thick bar across the exit as if to say no one else would leave until things were settled. One way or another.

Max heaved a sigh before turning back to Penelope. "The sheriff's here. If you really want to make it up to the pack, you'll confess."

Her wide-eyed gaze darted from one unfriendly face to the

next. "Wait a minute. I know what I did was wrong, but am I really taking all the blame?" She seemed floored by the unexpected development.

"Unfortunately, it looks that way. You can tell them Garrett was manipulating you, but they were still your actions."

"But I did it all for the pack. I did my best to make up for what I'd done."

Her desperate words brought to mind Zelda's pep talk. *You did the best you could in that moment.*

Penelope might have been trying her best, but what she couldn't see was the holding pattern she was stuck in, fixing one wrong with another while doubling down on her criminal activity. I recognized it because I'd also been trapped in a holding pattern for five years.

Even now, I was fixated on my guilt over leaving, locked in an emotional prison of my own making. But I couldn't rewrite the past through sheer desire alone, and no amount of self-punishment or reckless self-sacrifice would make up for what had happened. It was time to try something new before I dug myself into a hole so deep I couldn't see it for what it was, just like Penelope. It was time for acceptance.

I closed the space between us. "I understand, Penelope. You were alone, desperate to belong somewhere, and Garrett was dangling a carrot that would solve all your problems. You did your best. However, sometimes our best still has negative consequences, and we have to accept them. You can't change what you've done, and you certainly can't run from it, because you have an entire village who has heard your confession. But you have control over what you do next." I held her gaze. "What is the best you can do in this moment? What is the best you can do for this village?"

Defiance flickered across her features, followed by desperation and, finally, sadness. Her body sagged, and she covered her face with her hands. "Confess."

As she said it, her posture relaxed. Despite facing jail time, she seemed almost relieved, as though accepting what she couldn't change was a type of freedom in itself. And maybe, by accepting my own situation, I could finally find forgiveness—not from Max or even Nolan. To truly move on, I had to forgive myself.

The collective tension in the yurt unraveled. Max closed his eyes, chest deflating as if he'd been holding his breath. But the relief was short-lived when an insistent banging sounded against the wooden doors.

Max gestured for Teagan to open them. They swung wide, and I winced as light flooded the arena again. When my vision adjusted, I was staring at a red-faced Sheriff Reed. He planted his fists on his hips as he took in the scene: a sobbing Penelope, a half-naked and bleeding Max, and little old me smack dab in the middle of his investigation.

His wiry eyebrows drew together. "Miss Woods, what have you done now?"

CHAPTER TWENTY-FIVE

For once, I was actually happy when it was my turn to be interrogated by Sheriff Reed. It meant an escape from the stuffy confines of the yurt, where he'd asked us—or ordered us—to wait. Outside, the clouds still lingered, but the recent rain had brought a freshness that cleared the smell of body odor and blood from my nostrils while also clearing my mind.

When I'd finished my explanation, the sheriff gave me a dubious look before he consulted his notepad. "Let me see if I've got this straight. You drove all the way up here with Penelope, or Becky Rivers as she used to be called, and discovered she was the culprit behind everything. Then you simply asked her to confess?"

"Yes, but there was more to it than that." I shivered at the memory of the fight, at how close Max had come to defeat. It would haunt me forever.

He crossed his arms. "Enlighten me, then. What happened here today? Because no one else will give up the details." He gestured with his pen at the villagers gathered outside the yurt.

He was going to be sorely disappointed since I wasn't talking, either. "I just mean, there was detective work involved. But you'd know all about that, wouldn't you?" I gave him my most saccharine smile, feeling as though I'd earned it.

"And I'm supposed to accept all this at face value, when Max looks like he's been through a meat tenderizer after replacing Garrett as leader—who mysteriously disappeared?"

Okay, so that part did look pretty bad. "You have Penelope's full admission. Plus, the entire village has corroborated the story. And as far as how the murder weapon ended up in Max's truck, someone must have planted it there." As in Teagan, but I couldn't tell him a wolf did it.

"That part I can explain," he said. "Penelope admitted to planting it herself."

I blinked. "She did?"

"Apparently, she stashed it in his truck last night and deleted the security footage of the deed."

I considered the cruiser parked nearby, where Penelope hunched in the back seat. Was taking responsibility for Teagan's actions her way of making it up to Max? Or perhaps it was her loyalty to Truce, to the community she'd been so desperate to be a part of again. Either way, it tied up the one loose end that risked exposing the shifters.

"So I guess that solves everything." I slowly backed away. "If you have no further questions, am I free to go?"

"Now, hold on a minute." Reed held up a finger. "I wouldn't be doing my job if I ignored all the missing pieces."

I didn't blame him. While he'd technically gotten all the answers he needed, the strange circumstances would raise red flags for any good—or even mediocre—officer of the law. But those answers would only lead him to trouble.

"You know what they say, Sheriff. If you pull on a fin, you get a shark."

His cold blue eyes narrowed. "Is that a threat, Miss Woods?"

"No. It's a friendly warning. Truce doesn't like outsiders. You have your bad guy, so why keep digging? Unless you're determined to pin something on Max. He isn't guilty of anything now, and he wasn't guilty of the B and E. I think you know that, even if your pride won't let you admit it."

He sucked on his teeth as he pierced me with a frosty look. "Maybe it's not Max I want to investigate but you."

I was so tired of the sheriff's thinly veiled threats to uncover my secret. If a big, bad shifter leader was afraid of me, then the sheriff should be too.

"There are worse things than sharks in the ocean, Sheriff." Now, that was a threat, and I let it hang between us. "If you have no further questions…"

His mustache twitched with annoyance, but he finally pivoted and marched toward his cruiser.

Score one for me.

Before I could dwell on the school of fish I'd just disturbed, Jason strode over. As if to show he wanted to chat in an unofficial capacity, he removed his wide-brimmed hat and smoothed his blond hair.

"Are you okay?" he asked. "I was really worried when I heard you came here alone."

I wanted to point out I hadn't been so irresponsible as to come alone until I remembered my companion had, in fact, been the murderer. "I'm fine, thanks."

"Good. Here, take these." He tossed me the keys to the resort's SUV. "Trent will want his vehicle back, so you can follow us down the mountain. We don't have space in our cruiser, and I figure it's safer than you hanging around here until I can return for you." His focus homed in on something in the distance.

I didn't need to look to know he was staring at Max. "He's not the bad guy you believe he is."

"Maybe not this time." It seemed like he wanted to argue further but changed his mind. "We'll be leaving in ten if you want to follow us out."

"Thanks."

With a nod, I turned and made my way to the large group gathered outside the yurt. Max and I hadn't talked since the sheriff arrived, and while this wasn't the best time for a heart-to-heart, I wanted to at least say goodbye.

I was halfway there when Nolan sidled up to me. Thanks to the cloud cover, his smug look was hard to miss. "Another case closed, thanks to me. You should have brought me on your trip from the start."

That wasn't exactly my idea of a dream vacation, but I didn't tell him that. "I'm just glad you were able to help once you arrived. I knew you still cared about what happens to Max."

Shoving his hands into his ghostly suit pockets, he kicked at a rock as he walked. He missed, of course. "It's not that I didn't care from the start. It's just that… when I got to the resort and you were so intent on helping Max, it brought up a lot of feelings for me."

"What feelings?"

"I get jealous of you and Max sometimes."

My posture stiffened, but I kept my focus straight ahead. Did he suspect? "What about Max and me?"

"It used to be the three of us, you know? Now, I'm stuck watching you two hang out and solve cases together, moving on with your lives as if nothing happened."

Coming to a stop, I turned to face him. His pouty lip tugged at my heart. "That's not true at all, and you know it. Losing you changed us forever. It's what makes my friendship with Max even more important. The three of us made so many memories together, and I don't want to walk away from all of that."

The skin next to his eyes tightened as he studied me. "But that's all. Right? There's nothing else I need to be jealous about?"

His question harpooned me to the spot. While he'd asked it so casually, there was an intensity lurking beneath the question that frightened me, a hardness to his stare. It was so un-Nolan-like.

I returned it as steadily as I could. "Of course not. We're just friends." It was the truth. Because, despite any niggling hope residing in me, that hadn't changed. And something in Nolan's tense expression told me that so long as he was still around, nothing ever could.

He smiled, and I relaxed. My guilt must have been playing head games with me. Nolan had never been the jealous type. He was feeling left out. That was all.

Wanting to put the odd interaction behind us, I continued walking. "Come on. Now that this case is solved, I'll ask Max what he knows about yours. Just like I promised."

However, as I neared the villagers clustered around Max, all vying for his attention, I wondered if I had to take a number. I spotted Anita standing quietly at the edge of the crowd. She waved me over, and we waited for a pause in the onslaught of congratulatory hugs and handshakes for the new leader.

A moment later, the energy shifted abruptly, everyone falling silent until only the rustling of leaves and distant bird calls remained. I craned my neck to see past shifting bodies. Teagan was approaching Max, straight-backed, her lips forming a grim line as if bracing for her punishment.

"Teagan Ashwind." Max regarded her thoughtfully. "Your actions in the arena didn't go unnoticed. Thank you for your help. As a result, I'd like you to continue serving this community in the same capacity you did while under Garrett."

Her eyes widened. "But… But I set you up for murder."

"Only because Garrett took your loyalty for granted. And he had to lie to get you to comply because he knew you wouldn't obey otherwise. In the end, you did what was best for this community, not the leader. That's what I'm looking for in my team. Not someone who will follow my orders without question but who will take me to task if I get out of line." His lips twisted wryly. "And I think you're the best person for that job."

After a stunned moment, she dipped her head. "It would be an honor."

Shane pushed his way to the front of the group. Narrowing his close-set eyes at Teagan, he jabbed a finger in her direction. "You don't deserve the position. You betrayed the very leader you were supposed to protect."

She sized up the short-tempered man. "You want to talk betrayal? Garrett betrayed us all in conspiring with Penelope. And you betrayed us when you broke pack law and interfered in the fight."

"She's right." Max crossed his arms. "What do you have to say in your defense?"

Shane swallowed hard, as though the seriousness of his predicament had suddenly dawned on him. Without the leader's protection, he was no longer untouchable.

He sneered. "I don't need to defend myself to you, traitor."

Teagan darted forward and grabbed him by the shirt collar. "Watch how you talk to our leader!"

Max laid a hand on her shoulder. She let go of the muscular man and stepped aside. Shane tweaked his collar back into shape, appearing smug, until Max loomed over him.

"I am the leader now. That is our way. If you don't like it, you can challenge me or leave."

While he hadn't yelled, people around him cowered as if he had. I'd felt the effects too. A power that hadn't been there before. Whether it was a wolf thing or simply something he'd found within himself after all this time, I couldn't be sure. I was certain of one thing, though; this was no longer the same Max. This was an alpha.

Shane puffed up his chest. "Then I renounce my allegiance to the pack." He turned and stormed off into the woods, much like Garrett had.

Max simply watched him go.

I wondered if there would be a lot of changes in the community membership, with some folks leaving and others returning. Perhaps it was like this every time. It would certainly be a big change for everyone, especially since it wasn't an election but a leader forced on them. However, the majority of the pack seemed pleased. And why wouldn't they be? While anyone was better than Garrett, Max would be better than most.

As the tense atmosphere eased, Max approached me and his mother. Tutting at the sight of his shoulder wound, Anita took off her scarf and tried to dab away some of the blood.

He gently waved her off. "I'm all right."

"Of course you are." She beamed at him. "You're the leader. Just as you were meant to be. We'll all be all right now."

To my surprise, he really did look better. His wound had scabbed over, and the swelling to his eye had subsided, so I got the full force of his blue gaze as he fixed it on me.

I slipped his father's signet ring off my thumb and handed it to him with reverence. "I think you'll be needing this. You should know how proud your father is… was," I amended.

He stared down at it as though it held the answers to all life's questions, or at least the ones he wanted. "You sensed that through the ring?"

"I didn't have to. He was here."

Anita leaned away from me. "So you were being serious earlier? I thought you only said that to scare Garrett." She shivered, proving the tactic had worked on her too.

"Myles was really here," I told her before turning back to Max. "He has been all along, watching over you in his wolf form. He even helped me solve the case." I took in the revelers. "I think this is what he wanted for you, to see you rise to your full potential as leader, his people in good hands. After you won the fight, he moved on. He's finally at peace."

Max blinked rapidly before sliding the ring onto his finger. "I'll do my best to honor his memory."

"You already have," I said. "However, for a minute, I was worried you'd actually kill Garrett at the end of the fight."

"I wanted to." A flicker of rage passed over his face, so raw it frightened me. "But then, I wouldn't be any better than him. I did have to send him and all his supporters a message, though. I could leave no doubt who was boss."

"Well, boss. What happens now?"

He raised his uninjured shoulder. "I lead."

Teagan joined us, catching the last of our conversation. With a wide grin, she slapped him on the back. "No. Now, we celebrate."

I wrinkled my nose. "Really? After… well, everything that happened today?"

Her eyelids fluttered as if she were fighting back a flood of complex emotions. I couldn't imagine what she was experiencing. Relief her brother's killer was going to jail? Grief as she watched the pack move on without him? Perhaps even joy that Max was back. I wasn't sure how I felt about the last one.

With some effort, she stood straighter. "Of course. What better time than after hardship? A happy gathering after a change in leadership can help ease tensions. Watch this." She turned back to the throng, cupping a hand next to her mouth. "Who's ready to party?!"

The crowd erupted into cheers. Some people rushed off, already debating what dishes to bring to the feast, bickering over who made the juiciest roast and whose dessert always disappeared first. Others fist-bumped and high-fived, threatening to drink Max under the table.

It was such a strange energy after the seriousness of the day. My emotions were stretched thin after being pulled in so many directions. Was this what it had been like after Garrett killed Myles? People were ready to drink and dance the night away?

As I watched Max interact with the other villagers, it seemed he was struggling to muster enthusiasm for the celebration. Most people probably assumed he was tired after the fight. To me, his expression looked bittersweet.

My resolve to question him about Nolan faltered. The past few days had taken their toll. Having barely survived the investigation, the last thing I wanted to do was sit around and dredge up painful memories again. Something told me Max wouldn't be in the mood to either.

Next to me, Nolan watched on silently, focus shifting from me to Max. "Maybe now isn't the best time to ask about the accident. I've waited this long; I suppose I can wait a little longer."

Relief rushed through my veins. I wanted to help Nolan. Really, I did. But I simply needed time to recover. "Thank you."

Max cracked up at a group of rowdy revelers bumping chests then returned to me. "So, Vi. Will you stay for the party?"

I shook my head. "I don't think so. Someone has to drive Trent's SUV back to the resort, and Alice will be worried about me."

His bruised face creased with some emotion, and his Adam's apple bobbed before he plastered on a smile. "I understand. We'll catch up soon."

My throat suddenly felt thick, as though this were a goodbye instead of a see-you-later. "Of course."

After giving Anita one last hug, Nolan and I left Max to enjoy the festivities. Now that relief was sinking in and the fear for his life—and mine—had ebbed, an emptiness replaced it.

While I was happy for my friend, the adventure had started with my desire to get close to him again in whatever way I could, and his role as leader of a secluded and highly secretive village would only take him further away from me. Watching him settle into his new world, I wondered if I'd just lost him forever.

CHAPTER TWENTY-SIX

As Alice, Trent, and I walked toward the marina, where our ride awaited, I turned my face to the afternoon sun. The breeze was no stronger than a butterfly's wingbeat, so our trip home would be smooth sailing—or, I supposed, smooth speed-boating. A lot smoother than the weekend had been. Then again, things could have been worse.

After returning from Truce the day before, I'd yearned for my bed back in Hope, but there'd still been loose ends to tie up around the resort. Alice hadn't been in a rush to leave either. While she was being wined and dined by Trent during supper, I tracked down Levi and gave him the good news. It was hard to tell if his furry face showed signs of happiness—or if cats could feel anything close to it—but he finally moved on.

Thankfully, both Zelda and Nolan had caught a ride back to town early, allowing me to salvage what was left of my much-needed vacation. Using so much magic in such a short time had depleted me. It felt like I had a hangover. Perhaps magic was a muscle, and I'd been avoiding the gym for far too long. If I was going to keep getting tangled up in murder investigations, that would have to change.

After spending as much time as possible in the spa, I was

feeling a little better. My red waves had been tamed with a blowout, every kinked muscle had been massaged, and my freshly painted nails sparkled. As an inside joke, I'd chosen cardinal red.

When we reached the docks, I trailed behind Alice and Trent to give them space to say goodbye. With the grand opening still on, he'd be busy preparing, and she'd be in Hope, baking goods to send to the resort, so they wouldn't have much time together. Not until he hired a new assistant, anyway.

The marina was practically deserted, since most guests had scattered the second the sheriff announced the end of the investigation. Leonard Crab had been especially enthusiastic, claiming he was going to give the Shipwreck Shelter a fresh coat of paint as soon as he got back. Thanks to the distinct lack of boats, I had a clear view of the *Crescent* floating alone with the cabin door wide open. Max was back.

My insides cinched tight, and my footsteps slowed. "Alice, I'll meet you at the boat in a few minutes. I'm going to go say goodbye to Max."

"Take your time," she said dreamily, unable to take her eyes off Trent.

I beamed, happy for my friend, especially now that her new beau wasn't a murderer. "See you later, Trent. Thanks again for the hospitality."

He huffed. "Some hospitality. And I should be thanking you. Because of you, the resort will have a fighting chance. I just wish you'd had a better stay."

"Actually, all things considered, it was exactly what I needed." I waved and headed for the *Crescent*, realizing how true my response was.

Maybe I hadn't fully resolved things where Max was concerned, and I probably never would. In fact, I'd pushed him even farther away—as in all the way to Truce. But at least I'd helped him face his ghosts, in more ways than one. And the heaviness that pressed on my chest each time I saw him had eased, allowing me to breathe again. It was a step in the right direction.

When I boarded the *Crescent*, I peered inside the belly of the boat. Max stared up at me with a soft smile as if he'd been expecting my arrival. His shoulders lowered an inch, and his chest rose in a deep breath. I felt my body melt like silver under a torch as I climbed inside.

While I was tempted to take a seat and stay, my unsettling conversation with Nolan was still fresh in my mind. What if he hadn't gone back to town after all but was watching from shore? What would he think if I stayed too long?

Paranoid, I stood awkwardly by the stairs. "How was the celebration last night?"

"Good. Though I'm a bit tired today. I came back to grab some stuff and give Trent my notice. I'll be busy from now on, so I've asked a pack member to take over the maintenance work for me. He's a good contractor and has a crew that can rebuild the deck in time for next weekend. I even talked the inspector into assessing it ahead of the grand opening."

"I guess being a village leader has its perks." My throat tightened. "Sorry things turned out the way they did. I know you didn't want to be the leader."

He was shaking his head before I even finished, dark tendrils of hair brushing his nearly healed face. "Look, I was a hypocrite to judge you for leaving the island, because I was running from my own ghosts. Being leader feels right, and I owe you one for helping me figure that out."

"Since you stepping up as leader saved my life, we'll call it even."

He chuckled, but it quickly faded, and he grew serious. "I've been thinking a lot about yesterday and what you said to Penelope, about your best still having negative consequences. Were you talking about us? Did you go to Truce because you believed you needed to make up for something?" He held up his palms. "Don't get me wrong. I appreciate everything you did. I'm a free man because of you, but I never meant to put you in danger. And I'm sorry for it."

His face creased with guilt, and I was suddenly so tired of that feeling, of having it, of causing it. I sat on the built-in couch and patted the seat next to me. He joined me hesitantly as though steeling himself.

"For a long time, I held onto so much guilt for leaving. But I don't blame myself anymore. It was a difficult situation, and I did my best." I laid a hand over his, the gesture so familiar and yet somehow new. "Solving the case was about helping a friend because, while I might have left for five years, no amount of time would change how I feel about you."

As Max regarded me, I realized my words could be interpreted to mean either my feelings for him as a friend or the past romantic feelings I'd recently confessed to. I decided not to clarify.

I became overly aware my hand still lay over his. Slowly, he turned his palm upward, and his fingers curled until we were almost holding hands. It was such a subtle movement, and yet it made my head whirl with possibilities.

"Maybe…" he began. "Maybe when I'm free, we can go out to dinner. We've wasted enough time. Let's pick up where we left off."

Did he mean as friends? Or was he referring to the night he'd asked me to run away with him? Like my statement, it held two potential meanings, and I knew I'd spend the next several days trying to decipher it. But how could we ever be together when he lived in a remote community filled with people who were afraid of my powers? And if that didn't stop us, Nolan would.

I pulled away and hugged myself. "Part of the reason I came here was to ask about Nolan. There are still unanswered questions about that night."

Dropping his focus to the table, he drew back as if his best friend's name was a cold shower. "Is that why he hasn't moved on yet? Because of the accident?"

"That's the thing. We don't think it was an accident."

His face fell. "What do you mean? The sheriff said—"

"The sheriff." My laugh sounded hollow. "Reed concluded that either Nolan lost control of the car or there was a mechanical malfunction. It's not what happened, though." Unable to sit still, I stood to pace around the cramped cabin as I recalled the incident. "The car took over. The steering wheel moved all by itself, and no matter how hard Nolan hit the brakes, the engine revved, speeding us toward that curve. It's like it had a mind of its own."

He braced his elbows on the table and rubbed a hand over his mouth like he was going to be sick. "You think someone was behind it? That Nolan was murdered?"

"Yes. I wondered if you might have some insight into what happened, since you're mechanically inclined and worked on the car earlier that day. Not that I'm accusing you of doing anything to the car yourself," I rushed to explain.

His expression softened, and a weak smile tugged at his lips. "I don't think you would have put your life in danger to save me from jail if you believed I had." Then he frowned. "But when it left the garage that day, the car was in perfect working order. And I was the only one who went anywhere near it. If someone messed with it, they did it after it left the shop."

"Does it sound like anything you've ever heard of happening to a classic car?"

"No. But…" Max's eyes widened. He crossed the cabin and gripped me by the shoulders. "Are you sure Nolan was the target?"

A wave of numbness washed over me. "Why wouldn't he have been? It was his car."

His grasp tightened almost painfully. "He wasn't going to drive the car home that night. He planned to go back with his parents. The reason he had me give it a tune-up, the reason he drove it to the rehearsal dinner, was to give you the keys. He wanted you to show up to the wedding in style the next morning." He crushed me to his chest and spoke the next words into my hair. "You were supposed to be the only one in the car."

I felt breathless from both the shock and his desperate hold on me. "You mean someone wanted me dead?" Then another thought hit me. Did they still want me dead?

Max pulled away to meet my gaze. "Vi, I won't let anyone hurt you. I promise, we will find Nolan's murderer together so we can all finally move on."

His words filled me with both hope and dread. Hope for Nolan's closure, for a possible future together with Max. And dread that my investigation was going to be more deadly than I'd first imagined.

I hope you enjoyed reading *Inlaid to Rest*. If you have a moment, I would be so grateful if you could leave an honest review online. Reviews are crucial for any author, and even just a sentence or two can make a huge difference. I genuinely appreciate your time and support.

Thanks!
Casey

ACKNOWLEDGMENTS

Somehow, I managed to conjure up another book despite its best efforts to elude me. I definitely couldn't have done it without the support of my family and team, though. To Claire Taylor and Becca Syme, thank you for helping me find the diamond in the rough. Of course, it wouldn't shine as brightly without the magical editing of Dayna M. Reidenouer and Kimberly Husband. And I'm so grateful to my beta readers—Bree Rich, Claire Merle, Veronica McIntyre, and Caitlyn Lynn—for their pearls of wisdom. Thank you, everyone, for a spooktacular experience.

ABOUT THE AUTHOR

Casey Griffin spent her childhood dreaming up elaborate worlds and characters. Now, she writes those stories down. As a jack-of-all-trades, her résumé includes registered nurse, heavy equipment operator, English teacher, photographer, and pizza delivery driver. She's a world traveler and has a passion for anything geeky. With a wide variety of life experiences to draw from, she loves to write stories that transport readers and make them smile. Casey lives in Southern Alberta with her family, and when she's not traveling, attending comic conventions, or watching *Star Wars*, she's writing every moment she can.

CASEYGRIFFIN.COM